WILLIAM AND THE MOON ROCKET

"WHO'S THIS BOY?" ASKED THE COLONEL'S WIFE, MAKING
A LUNGE AT WILLIAM AS HE DODGED PAST HER.

(*See page* 161)

WILLIAM AND THE MOON ROCKET

BY
RICHMAL CROMPTON

ILLUSTRATED BY
THOMAS HENRY

LONDON
GEORGE NEWNES LIMITED
TOWER HOUSE, SOUTHAMPTON STREET
STRAND, W.C.2

First Published	.	.	*1954*
Second Impression	.	.	*1955*
Third Impression	.	.	*1957*

Printed in Great Britain by
Wyman & Sons, Ltd., London, Fakenham and Reading

CONTENTS

CHAPTER I

WILLIAM AND THE MOON ROCKET

"WE'VE got to be first on the moon," said William with an air of stern determination.

"What d'you mean, first on the moon?" said Ginger.

The two were sitting astride the roof of the toolshed, idly surveying the landscape. They had begun by pretending that they were shipwrecked mariners astride a raft and, when that palled, had become the occupants of a comet soaring through space. It was too hot to do anything more active.

"Well, someone's got to be first on the moon," said William.

"We couldn't *really*," said Ginger, who was always slightly disconcerted by William's swift transitions from make-believe to reality.

"I don't see why not," said William. "I tell you, *someone*'s got to do it an' I don't see why it shouldn't be us. Think of all the things we might have found if someone else hadn't found 'em first—electricity an' television an'—an' potato crisps an' gorgeous technicolor an'"—in a tone of deep disgust—"Everest. Gosh! I'd like to've been the first up Everest. I bet I could've been, too, if I'd had a chance. It's jus' climbin' an' I bet I can climb as well as anyone. I've climbed to the top of mos' of the trees round here. I bet if all the climbin' I've ever done was put together it'd reach to the top of Everest. An' if they want a sledge dog there's Jumble. He's jolly good at sledgin', is Jumble. He pulled that sledge of provisions when we were playin' at findin' the North Pole."

"Yes, but he ate all the provisions," Ginger reminded him.

"Oh, well," said William, "he was hungry. He knew he'd got to keep his strength up to pull the sledge."

"Not much point in pullin' the sledge when he'd ate all the provisions off it," said Ginger.

"Anyway, it was a jolly good expedition," said William, avoiding further discussion of his pet's rôle as a husky, "an' I bet we'd have done it jus' as well in real life."

"Well, it's no good worryin' over Everest now," said Ginger. "We're too late. It's been climbed."

"No, but the moon's left," said William.

"What d'you mean, the moon's left?" said Ginger.

"Gosh, why don't you *listen*?" said William irritably. "I've been *talkin*' about it, haven't I? I keep tellin' you, *someone*'s got to get to the moon first an' I don't see why it shouldn't be us."

"We've not got a rocket," said Ginger.

"Well, we could make one, couldn't we?" said William.

"No," said Ginger simply, "an' we couldn't get any atom stuff to shoot it off either."

William considered this in silence for some moments.

"I bet that atom stuff isn't all that necess'ry," he said at last. "I bet there's lots of diff'rent ways of shootin' people to the moon. I bet if you got a strong enough spring . . ."

"We don't know where it is," said Ginger. "The moon, I mean."

" 'Course we do," said William. "Are you *blind* or somethin'? Gosh! You can *see* the moon any night. All you've got to do is to wait till it's dark an' *aim* at it. I'm a jolly good shooter. I hit that apple I was aimin' at with my catapult jus' now an' I bet if I can hit a little thing like an apple I can hit a big thing like the moon. If I got the right sort of spring to shoot at it. . . ."

"You didn't hit that tree you were tryin' to hit this morning," said Ginger, who was occasionally only very occasionally—stung to protest by William's assumption of omnipotence. "You're a rotten shot."

"I'm not."

"You are."

"Say it again."

"You're a rotten shot."

There was a short scuffle and both of them rolled down from the tool-shed roof to the ground.

"I'd meant to get down, anyway," said William with dignity, picking himself up and brushing garden soil from his person. "Let's go to the village an' have a look at the sweet shop."

"Have you got any money?"

"No. Have you?"

"No."

"That doesn't matter. We'll go 'n' choose what we'd buy if we'd got some."

The two strolled slowly down towards the village, kicking stones, scrambling in and out of the ditch and keeping up a desultory conversation.

"Gosh! I bet that's a rat . . . No, it isn't. It's a frog."

"Wonder what sort of houses they live in. On the moon, I mean. "

"I bet they don't live in houses at all . . . Here's a jolly good caterpillar, but I've got enough hairy ones, so I'm letting it go . . . I bet they live in trees or in caves. I'm goin' to live in a cave. I'm goin' to have a jolly big one with pools of water in it an' I'm goin' to tame some of their wild animals to live in it with me."

"P'r'aps there aren't any wild animals there."

"There's always wild animals in undiscovered places. There was polar bears at the North Pole an'—an' zebras somewhere. I've forgotten where . . . Gosh! Here's a banana skin in the ditch. It's got a bit of banana left in the end. An' there's a lot on the sides, too."

"Wait a minute," said Ginger, dragging a battered note-book and pencil from his pocket. "There's a car coming an' I want to get its number."

Ginger had recently taken up the hobby of car number collecting and recorded the number of each car he noticed on the road with painstaking thoroughness. His aim was to record a hundred in one day, but so far he had only reached a total of twenty-nine.

William looked on the hobby with disfavour. It seemed to him devoid of dramatic possibilities and he did his best to discourage Ginger's interest in it.

"You're too late now," he said coldly. "I've ate all I could get off."

"I don't care," said Ginger, replacing the book in his pocket. "That's my thirteenth and a half today. I'm countin' the one I didn't see the end of as a half . . . What sort of a rocket are we going to the moon in?"

"We'll have think that out."

"It'll take a bit of thinkin'!"

William put his hands in his pockets and swaggered on airily down the road.

"I gen'rally get ideas for things. I get jolly good ideas. I got a jolly good idea for turnin' that ole birdbath into a fountain."

"It didn't work. It jus' made us drippin' wet an' then dried up."

"Well, that didn't stop it bein' a good idea," said William unabashed.

They were passing the Red Lion and paused to watch a lorry, laden with complicated pieces of machinery, that had just drawn up at the entrance.

A man got down from the driving seat and stood contemplating the flat tyre of one of the front wheels. He was a small, ferret-faced man with sandy hair and eyebrows.

"Puncture," he said, with the air of one who sums up a weighty situation.

A peaky-looking youth, who was passing on a motor-cycle, dismounted.

"Like a hand?" he said.

In silence the two changed the wheel, watched with tense interest by William and Ginger.

Then they stood, wiping their hands on grease-stained rags, inspecting their handiwork.

"That's fixed it," said the youth.

"Yip," said the man. He jerked his head in the direction of the inn. "Time fer 'arf a pint? I ain't got much time meself." He jerked his head in the direction of the lorry. "Got to take that there moon rocket over to Biggleswick."

The two disappeared into the Red Lion.

William and Ginger stared at each other. Their mouths had dropped open.

"Gosh!" said William hoarsely. "Did you hear what he said? It's a *moon rocket*!"

Ginger was gazing at the machinery with an awe-struck look on his face.

"I didn't know they'd axshully started makin' 'em yet," he said.

"I bet it's the first one," said William. "I bet it's the first one that's ever been made."

Ginger walked round the lorry, examining its load.

"It doesn't look like what I thought a moon rocket'd look like," he said.

"Well, that's what I *said*," said William, his excitement rising. "I *said* there mus' be lots of diff'rent ways of gettin' there."

"I wonder which part they axshully shoot to the moon," said Ginger.

"I bet that's the one," said William, pointing to a large cylinder that towered over the rest of the metal pieces. "I bet——" He stopped short and gave a gasp. His face had paled with excitement. "*Gosh! I've got an idea!*"

"What?" said Ginger.

"Let's get inside it. It's jolly big. We can both get into it easy. Let's get inside it an' go wherever it's goin'. We may get shot to the moon in it. They may fix it up an' shoot it off without noticin' we're in it an'—an' we'll get first to the moon, same as I said we would."

Ginger considered.

"Um-m . . . We might. It's worth tryin'."

" 'Course it is," said William. He looked up and

down the empty road. "Come on quick while there's no one about."

It was the work of a few seconds to scramble up into the lorry and make their way into the recesses of the cylinder.

"It's not very comfortable," said Ginger, trying to accommodate his person to the hard curves of his hiding-place.

"Well, you don't want to be *comfortable*, goin' to the moon," said William severely. "If you wanted to be comfortable, you ought to've stayed at home."

"'I bet I'll wish I had done, before we've finished," said Ginger. "I'm getting all over oil, too. It's jolly oily in here."

"What's a bit of oil?" said William. "I bet those people that discovered the North Pole an' Everest an' —an' gorgeous technicolour didn't mind a bit of oil. Here! Move your leg away. It's right in my face."

"Well, your face is takin' up all the room. You——"

"Shut up! He's comin' back."

The ferret-faced man and peaky-looking youth were emerging from the inn. The youth mounted his motor-cycle and disappeared down the road. The ferret-faced man hoisted himself into the driver's seat and started the engine. The van moved off and gathered speed.

For some moments William and Ginger remained tense and silent; then, by degrees, they relaxed (as far as relaxation was possible in the constricted space) and began to converse in whispers.

"We ought to've brought provisions," said Ginger.

"We'll find somethin' on the moon," William reassured him. "There's people on the moon an' they mus' eat. We'll jus' have to eat what they eat."

"As long as it's not tapioca pudding," said Ginger anxiously. He had a particular aversion to that form of nourishment.

"P'r'aps it'll be ice-cream an' bananas an' lollypops," said William. "Or p'r'aps it'll be somethin' nicer than anythin' we've ever tasted before."

THE MAN CARRIED THE CARTONS INTO
THE RAMSHACKLE SHED.

They were silent for a few moments, giving themselves up to rapt contemplation of this possibility.

"He's goin' a long way," said Ginger at last.

"Well, he would to get to the moon," said William.

"I mean, he'd have to get to a very far-off sort of place to shoot the rocket—or whatever it is—'cause he'd nat'rally want to keep it secret."

"If he wanted to keep it secret," said Ginger after a short pause, "why did he tell the other man?"

"P'r'aps he was a confederate," said William, "or p'r'aps he jus' forgot it was a secret. It's jolly easy to forget somethin's a secret. I've done it myself."

"How're we goin' to get back?" said Ginger. "From the moon, I mean."

"I bet we'll find some way," said William. "It's always easier gettin' down from a place than gettin' up to it. I shouldn't mind stayin' there, anyway. We wouldn't have to go to school."

"He's not stoppin' yet," said Ginger. "He's goin' a jolly long way."

The lorry sped on and on—through villages and towns, along country roads, over commons and heathlands. Suddenly it drew up alongside another lorry.

Ginger, peering out of the cylinder, automatically pulled his note-book from his pocket and noted the number of the second lorry.

Wonderingly, the two boys watched the ferret-faced man get down from his lorry, take several large cartons from the second lorry, assisted by its driver, transfer them to his own lorry (William and Ginger drew their heads in quickly at this point), then return to his driving-seat and restart his engine. Not a word had been spoken during the transaction. The lorry sped on again.

"Wonder what was in those boxes," said Ginger.

"Provisions, prob'ly," said William. "There might be the sort of food on the moon that you can't eat."

"Tapioca pudding," said Ginger.

"Anyway, I bet it's provisions."

"Hope it's somethin' good," said Ginger with a note of relish in his voice. "They're near my side so I could jus' creep out an' have a look."

"Don't start eatin' it," said William sternly. "We don't want to get to the moon an' then find we've nothin' to eat. We'd feel jolly silly gettin' to the moon on' then havin' to starve to death."

"I'll only look," promised Ginger.

He crawled out of the cylinder, approached the cartons, lifted the lids and returned.

"They're cigarettes," he said in a mystified voice, handing William a couple of cigarettes. "I took these out to show you."

"P'r'aps they're for him to smoke when he gets to the moon," said William uncertainly.

"He'd never want all that lot. There mus' be *thousands*."

"P'r'aps he's going to give 'em to the natives to buy food with. People used to buy things with cigarettes in the war." But this explanation seemed too tame. He examined the cigarettes more carefully. "I don't believe they *are* cigarettes."

"They look like 'em an' they smell like em," said Ginger.

"Yes, I know they do," said William. "I bet that's what's so clever about them. I bet they're for shootin' the rocket to the moon. I bet they're sort of little atom sticks. He doesn't want anyone to know he's goin' to the moon, so he's had 'em made to look like cigarettes. He'll make a pile of 'em an' set 'em off an' they'll shoot the rocket up to the moon. I bet he's a jolly clever man. He *looks* a jolly clever man. He——"

"He's stoppin' again," said Ginger in a warning voice.

The lorry was drawing up at a large ramshackle shed by the roadside. Again the two heads peeped cautiously out of the cylinder as the man got down from the driving-seat, unlocked the padlock of the shed, lifted down the cartons, carried them into the shed, relocked the padlock, returned to the driving-seat and started the engine again.

"What did he do that for?" said Ginger.

"I bet I know," said William. "Did you see that little hill behind the shed? It had a sort of crooked little tree growin' on it. I bet that tree sort of points at the moon an' he's goin' to use it to help him take aim at it. He's goin' to fix the rocket to the tree somehow to get it set off at the right angle."

"Well, why's he drivin' on then?"

"He's probably got some other things to fetch. Anyway, he won't do it till it's dark an' he can see the moon. He——" He stopped short with an ejaculation of amazement.

The lorry was turning into the gate of a large field— a field full of caravans and half-erected stalls and roundabouts. Groups of spectators had gathered round each and a policeman stood by the gate, watching proceedings with an air of dignity and boredom.

A small stout man with a couple of moon daisies in his buttonhole approached the lorry.

"Got it all right?" he said.

"Yip," said the ferret-faced man.

The small stout man turned to the little crowd of onlookers.

"Moon Rocket went out of action down in Hastings," he said genially. "Didn't know whether we'd get the parts back in time but seems we just done it. It's the up-to-date touch, is the Moon Rocket, Dodgems an' High Flyers an' Fun Swirls is all very well, but it's the Moon Rocket strikes the topical note. A fair ain't a fair these days without a Moon Rocket." He walked round the lorry. "Goin' to be a job, settin' it up again. Won't be able to open with it tonight . . . Well, get it shifted, lads."

Several men climbed on to the lorry and began to move the machinery. Two of them took up the cylinder, then set it down again.

"Blimey!" said one. "It ain't 'arf 'eavy."

William and Ginger had crept into the middle of their hiding-place and were trying to make themselves as small as possible.

The two men made another effort.

Suddenly one of them gave a yell.

"There's somethin' movin' inside of it," he said.

"Crikey, yes!" said the other. "Somethin' alive."

The bystanders gathered round the lorry. The policeman dropped his air of boredom and joined the little group.

"What's all this?" he said.

"Somethin' movin' in that there cylinder."

"Somethin' alive."

"A lion, as like as not," said a woman in a large black hat trimmed with feathers.

"Stand back there," said the policeman. He turned to the stout man with the buttonhole. "Have any of your animals escaped?"

"No," said the man. "We ain't got all that amount of animals."

"Seals, it looks like," said a tall woman, peering over the heads of the crowd into the recesses of the cylinder.

"It ain't Bill an' Susy," said a man with a flowing moustache and a striped pullover. "I jus' left 'em 'avin' their bath."

"Lions," persisted the woman in the feather-trimmed hat.

A man who had been setting up a hoop-la stall

approached with a long pole and stuck it into the cylinder.   A prolonged yell followed.

"Hyenas," said the woman with the feather-trimmed hat.

"Yuman," pronounced the policeman.   "Stand back, there."

The hoop-la man rammed the pole again into the cylinder . . . and out rolled two small boys, oil-blackened and grimy, falling from the cylinder on to the lorry and from the lorry on to the ground.

"Well, I'll be blowed!" said the policeman, momentarily forgetting his dignity.   "Stand *back*, there! . . . Now what have you two got to say for yourselves?"

Confused explanations poured from the oil-blackened forms.

"You see, we'd missed Everest . . ."

"An' we didn't want to miss the moon . . ."

"We heard him say it was a moon rocket . . ."

"We wanted to be first on it . . ."

"We thought those cigarettes he took off the other lorry . . ."

"I got its number.   It's my fourteenth an' a half today . . ."

"The ones he put in the shed.   Well, I thought they were atom sticks. . . ."

"What shed?" said the policeman.

"The shed with that hill an' that crooked tree behind it."

"It's the shed on the Minster road," said someone.

"It's where I keeps me lorry," stuttered the driver. His face had taken on a greenish hue.   "It's me own place, ain't it?   I've a right goin' in me own place, 'aven't I?"

THE FERRET-FACED MAN MADE A DASH FOR THE EXIT, BUT
THE POLICEMAN WAS TOO QUICK FOR HIM.

The policeman advanced towards him in a casual unconcerned fashion. He was an intelligent young man and had gathered more from the confused account than might have seemed possible.

"I'd like to know more about those cigarettes," he said, "and that other lorry."

The ferret-faced man turned and made a dash for the exit, but the policeman was too quick for him. He caught him up at the gate and secured him in an expert grasp.

"Take it easy," he said reassuringly as he tightened his grip on the wriggling form. "We only want to ask you a few straightforward questions. If you got straightforward answers to 'em you got nothing to worry about. Just come along to the station. It's a bit more private there. You two nippers hang round for a bit, will you?"

The stout little man turned to William and Ginger.

"Come and have an ice-cream," he said, "and let's hear all about it."

"He was the local carrier, you see, so no one suspected him," said the stout little man to Mr. Brown, "and it seems he'd been in league with these warehouse thieves for some time. They used to do a job, meet him at a certain spot and shift the stuff on to his lorry and he'd take it to this old shed where he kept his lorry. Full of the stuff, they found it. Hid under the floor-boards and everywhere. Up to the neck in it, he was. Being a local carrier, he could go up and down the country and no one could prove he wasn't on a job. And he was on jobs more often than not. That Moon Rocket was an O.K. job. I wanted the stuff brought straight from the factory down to Biggleswick, so I got a Biggleswick carrier to do it to save time. Came too late to open with it last night but it'll be O.K. tonight."

Mr. Brown listened with polite interest. He had heard the story several times before—from the police, from William, from Ginger, from most of the fair-ground men and from several of the onlookers.

"Observant kids," went on the stout little man. "Taking that lorry's number and giving a description of where the shed was on the Minster road. Tied things up a treat, that did." He looked down at William and Ginger, who were walking on either side of Mr. Brown. "Did a fine job, they did."

"More by good luck than good management," said Mr. Brown dryly.

"Glad you could come along, anyway," said the stout little man.

When William and Ginger received the invitation to be the first passengers on the newly-set-up Moon Rocket at the Biggleswick Fair, Mr. Brown had at first refused to allow the expedition, but his refusal was little more than a form and he was soon persuaded not only to give permission but to accompany them himself. He was at heart a simple man and he had always had a weakness for country fairs. Moreover, the Moon Rocket was new since his youth and he was secretly anxious to sample it.

"This way," said the stout little man, ushering them through an entrance which proclaimed: "Moon Rocket. Stupendous Adventure. Five Minutes of Unforgettable Thrills" over the doorway.

They entered and took their seats in a small compartment with cellophane windows.

MR. BROWN, WILLIAM AND GINGER AFTER A
PROFITABLE HOUR AT THE FAIR!

The door was closed and, to the accompaniment of a
deafening siren, the compartment rocked wildly then
seemed to shoot through the air. After that came the
five minutes of unforgettable thrills—swoops up and
plunges down—somersaults in which all three fell on
top of each other—strange scenes flashing past the
windows—men with heads where their feet should be
and feet where their heads should be—fantastic hills
and valleys—animals with lions' heads and crocodiles'
tails—strange trees bearing fruit that looked like giant
feather-dusters, wreathed by snakes with huge staring
eyes and pointed ears—more swoops and plunges and
somersaults—till at last, dazed and shaken, they
emerged once more into the open air.

"Grand, wasn't it?" said the stout little man.

"Wizard," said William.

"Super," said Ginger.

"Certainly unforgettable," said Mr. Brown.

"Not another to touch it in the length and breadth of England," said the stout little man.

"An'—gosh! We were the first in it," said William, looking at the long queue outside the entrance.

"It was extremely kind of you," said Mr. Brown. "And now, boys, we must be going home."

"Let's go out by the other gate," said William guilefully.

The way to the other gate led past the hoop-la stalls, the Wild Sea Waves, the big roundabout and most of the main attractions of the fair.

They reached the gate about an hour later.

Mr. Brown wore a bland triumphant air and carried a coco-nut under each arm. William held a couple of toffee apples in each hand and clasped to his breast a goldfish in a glass bowl. Ginger was nibbling a huge pyramid of candy floss. A purple balloon, secured to a button of his coat, floated over his head.

Dusk was falling and a full moon shone down serenely through the over-hanging trees.

William looked at it and heaved a wistful sigh.

"We never got there, after all," he said.

Ginger was sated with popcorn, toffee apples and candy floss; he had been whirled about on Dodgems, High Flyers and roundabouts; he was in a pardonable state of confusion.

He threw a careless glance at the golden disc and shrugged his shoulders.

"I don't care what it's like," he said. "It couldn't be as good as the real one."

CHAPTER II

WILLIAM AND THE NEW GAME

M RS. BROWN walked slowly away from the
Women's Institute meeting, where she had been
listening to a lecture on Child Management.

It had been an interesting lecture and she was
turning it over in her mind.

Beside her walked Mrs. Gilbert, a newcomer to the
neighbourhood, who had recently taken a house at the
further end of the village.

"She was a good speaker, wasn't she?" said Mrs.
Brown. She sighed. "And she made it sound so
simple."

"Yes . . . and it isn't really, is it?"

"No," said Mrs. Brown.

"I've got a girl of nine," said Mrs. Gilbert. "It's a
difficult age."

"I've got a boy of eleven," said Mrs. Brown, adding
with another sigh: "That's a difficult age, too."

"Still, I think that some of the things she said were
very helpful," said Mrs. Gilbert. "You remember,
she said that if ever we had to leave a child alone in the
house when we went out, we should make a sort of
game of it. Pretend to *give* the house for the time
we have to be away. Last week Patsy had a dreadful
cold and I had to slip out to the shops and leave her
and she was very sulky about it. If I'd made a game
of it and pretended to *give* her the house. . . ."

"Y-yes," said Mrs. Brown. "And that other suggestion about the Houses of Parliament."

"I've forgotten that . . . I was wondering whether Patsy was 'maladjusted,' and whether I dare ask exactly what it meant."

"Well, she said that boys got into mischief because they hadn't enough to occupy their minds and that we should lead them to take an interest in politics; and she suggested that we should encourage them to form a sort of 'Houses of Parliament' among themselves on the lines of the one at Westminster and study political questions and make speeches. It sounded all right when she said it. But"—doubtfully—"I don't know. . . ."

"I wonder whether she's got any children," said Mrs. Gilbert.

"Yes, I was wondering that," said Mrs. Brown. "Still, I think I'll try this Houses of Parliament idea with William. It can't do any harm. I'll wait till he shows signs of getting into mischief again."

She had not long to wait.

It was the next day that William "borrowed" his father's razor to assist him in the process of grafting a gooseberry bush on to a holly tree. Mr. Brown used an old-fashioned razor and took a pride in its state of shining keenness. In vain did William point out that a holly tree covered with gooseberries in the front garden would have increased their prestige among the neighbours and even perhaps brought them international fame. The house was filled with the tempest of Mr. Brown's wrath and when it died away it left William in a chastened mood. He received Mrs. Brown's suggestion with an air of docility.

B

"You see, dear," she said, "you and your friends can form a sort of Houses of Parliament and—well," vaguely, "pretend to be Ministers of the Crown and that sort of thing and—and discuss politics."

"Yes," said William and added with rising interest, "yes, it's a jolly good idea."

Mrs. Brown stifled a slight feeling of misgiving.

"You mustn't turn it into anything *rough*," she admonished. "It's just a quiet game to occupy your minds and lead your interest towards politics. A sort of *educational* game."

"Yes," said William. The thoughtful look on his face had deepened, and he was obviously giving earnest consideration to the suggestion. "Yes," he repeated, "I think we could make a jolly good game out of it. I'll c'lect the others an' we'll have a try."

A few minutes later he was setting off down the road. Mrs. Brown watched him from the window. He looked neat and tidy, he walked in a fashion that was almost decorous, but the slight feeling of misgiving still lingered.

"Oh, well," she reassured herself as she settled down to her basket of household mending, "a game like that can't possibly lead to any harm."

When William collected the other three Outlaws, the new game was at first overshadowed by the fact that Ginger had that morning received a belated birthday present of ten shillings from a godmother.

"Gosh!" said William excitedly. "What'll we spend it on?"

It was the Outlaws' custom to pool their tips. The actual recipient of the tip kept a restraining hand on the expenditure, but there his function ended.

"We're not goin' to go spendin' it all at once," said

Ginger firmly. "If we spend a bit every day it'll last for weeks an' *weeks*. It's a jolly lot of money, is ten shillings."

"Tell you what!" said Douglas. "I was in Marleigh with my mother yesterday an' they'd got some smashin' lollypops in the sweet shop there. They were made of rock—red an' white—and they looked wizard. They were bigger than ordin'ry lollypops an' they were only threepence each. I'd have bought one but I hadn't any money."

"Come on!" said the others shortly.

They hurried to Marleigh by the short cut across the fields, skirting the pond in a hit-or-miss fashion that spattered them with mud to their waists, scrambling through the hedge with an impetus that scratched their faces and dishevelled their hair, presenting themselves at the Marleigh sweet shop, towsled and grubby and so breathless that at first they could only pant.

"If you want to buy anythin', buy it," said the owner of the shop, eyeing them with disfavour, "an', if you don't, clear out."

"Yes, we do," said Ginger, recovering his breath. "We want"—he brought out his order triumphantly—"eight of those rock lollypops."

"Gosh!" said the other three ecstatically.

"An' I could buy more if I wanted to," went on Ginger, laying his ten-shilling note on the counter with an air of affluence. "I bet there's not many people about with all that money."

"All right, all right, all right!" said the man, handing him the lollypops and the change. "Bloomin' capitalists, the lot of you! Now clear off before I set the Income Tax bloke on you."

Ginger counted his change with an expression of deep suspicion and the four went out into the road, each holding lollypops in both hands and licking them alternately.

"We'll go back by the road," said Ginger. "We don't want to risk losin' 'em in the hedge or the pond."

"They're jolly good," said Douglas indistinctly, removing his lollypop stick carefully from his mouth.

"Well, don't go sucking them," said Ginger disapprovingly. "They last longer with licks."

"How much money have we got left?" said Henry.

"Eight shillings," said Ginger, "an' we're not goin' to spend any more today. We've got to make it last."

"Well, what'll we do now?" said Henry.

William gave each of his lollypops an all-embracing lick before he answered.

"My mother was s'gestin' a game this mornin' an' it sounded a jolly good one. She said we could play at bein' the Houses of Parliament."

"That doesn't sound much fun," said Ginger. "I'd sooner play at bein' Indians an' Cowboys than houses. Houses don't *do* anythin'."

"Don't be such a chump. This is *diff'rent*," said William. "We'd be the *people* in the Houses of Parliament. We'd carry on same as they do. They've all got diff'rent politics an' one lot tries to do things an' the other lots all try to stop 'em."

"Sounds rather fun," said Ginger thoughtfully. "What are they called?"

"I know all about that," said Henry, picking up his lollypop, which he had dropped in the road, and licking the dust off. "There's the Prime Minister an' the Whip an' a man called the Black Rod."

"Why?" said Douglas.

"He's the chucker-out. He chucks 'em out when they start fightin'."

"I told you it was a jolly good game," said William, adding complacently: "It's educational, too, so that makes it all right, whatever happens."

"I bet it'll get us in a muddle," said Douglas.

"No, it won't," said William. "I tell you, it's educational. Same as sums an' geography but a bit more excitin'."

"How do we start?" said Henry.

"Well, we've got to find a house to have the Houses of Parliament in first."

"Why not the old barn?" said Ginger.

"I think we'd better keep off the old barn today," said William regretfully. "Old Jenks is workin' in the field jus' next it an' he's been after us ever since we practised glidin' from his hay rick."

"We didn't do it any harm."

"No, an' I nearly broke my neck, but he didn't care about *that*. He wouldn't care if I had to go about with a broken neck for the rest of my life. . . . Anyway, we won't go to the old barn while he's working there."

"Where shall we go, then? . . . Gosh! My rock's come unstuck."

"You're lickin' too hard. . . . We'll have to find a house. We ought to have more than one to call it the *Houses* of Parliament, but we'll manage with one."

"Yes, an' how'll we find one?" said Henry. "It isn't so easy, findin' houses."

"FIVE SHILLINGS!" EXPLODED WILLIAM. "WE AREN'T
GOING TO PAY ALL THAT FOR IT."

William glanced at the houses that bordered the
road along which they were walking.

"There's lots about," he said carelessly.

"Yes, but there's people livin' in them," Ginger
pointed out.

"There's lors about houses," said Henry darkly.
"Some people can't get in 'em an' some people can't
be got out of 'em.   It's not so easy."

But William's optimism was not to be dispelled.

"I bet I get one," he said, licking the last vestiges

of lollypop from a stick before he threw it away. "I bet I get one all right."

"I bet you don't," said Douglas, "an' I bet even if you do it'll get us in a muddle."

"All right. You wait an' see. You——"

He stopped short.

They were passing a house in front of which a spreading elm tree grew from the centre of a small lawn. A little girl stood at the gate. She had a thin freckled face with two short pigtails sticking out from her head. Her expression was one of acute boredom, but her eyes gleamed avidly as they fell upon the red and white lollypops, whose remains the Outlaws were still licking with slow relish.

"Where did you get those?" she demanded unceremoniously.

"Fancy you not knowin' that!" said William, adopting a man-of-the-world swagger. "At the sweet shop in Marleigh, of course. Don't you know *any-thin'*?"

"'Course I do. . . .   What's your name?"

"Mind your own business," said William, but there was something about the little girl that impressed him, despite himself, and he added, "William Brown. What's yours?"

"Patsy Gilbert. . . .   How much are they?"

"Threepence each.   You could go over an' buy one if you wanted.   It doesn't take long by the short cut."

The little girl gave a shrug, eloquent of resignation and disgust.

"I haven't got threepence.   I haven't had any money since Saturday.   I spent it all on a balloon and it burst the next day."

"They always do," said Ginger.   "You were a chump to buy it."

The little girl looked from one to another of the Outlaws with gloomy interest.

"Where are you going?" she said.

"We're looking for a house," answered William importantly.

"What d'you want a house for?"

"Never you mind," said William, feeling that he had already shown himself over-friendly to this member of a despised sex.   "You jolly well mind your own business."

"You can have this house," said the little girl carelessly, "if you'll let me have some money to buy some lollypops like what you've got."

William was slightly—very slightly—taken aback.

"It's not yours to give," he said.

"I'm not going to give it you," said the little girl

tartly. "I'm going to *sell* it you. And it *is* mine. My mummy gave it me. She had to go into the village to get something 'cause Cousin Gertrude's coming, and she said, 'I'll give you the house, Patsy. Now remember, it's *your* house.' So you see, it *is* mine an' I *can* sell it."

"Oh . . ." said William. His eyes travelled to the house. It was a fair-sized comfortable-looking house. "How much d'you want for it?"

"How much have you got?" said Patsy.

"We've got eight shillings," said Ginger, "but we're not payin' all that jus' for a house."

"Well, how much *will* you pay, then?" said Patsy.

"You can get two of those lollypops for sixpence," said William.

"Well, I want more than two," said Patsy. "And it's a nice house. It's got an apple tree in the back garden with a swing hanging from it and it's got a ladder up into the loft and you can play with the water tank. It's worth more than sixpence."

"Well, we'll give you two shillings," said William. "You can buy eight lollypops with that and—gosh! eight lollypops ought to be enough for anyone. It's more than we've had."

"I'll sell it you for five shillings," said the little girl.

"Five shillings!" exploded William. "We aren't going to pay all that for it."

"All right. You can't have it," said the little girl, turning to go indoors.

William hesitated, then surrendered.

"All right," he said. "We'll give you five shillings for it."

Ginger counted out the money grudgingly.

"That only leaves us three shillings," he said. "It's goin' jolly quick."

The little girl took the money and put it into her blazer pocket.

"Where's this short cut to Marleigh?" she said in a business-like voice.

"You go over the stile and across the field and through the wood," said William. "Then there's another field on the other side of the wood with a pond at the end an' you can't get round one side of the pond 'cause it's all bog but you can get round it the hedge side if you keep right close to the hedge an' then there's another field and you can get through the hedge at the end of that one into the road an' the sweet shop's jus' there."

The little girl did not seem intimidated or bewildered by these directions. She buttoned her blazer about her and set off jauntily down the road.

The Outlaws entered the gate and stood for a moment inspecting their purchase with the pride of ownership while they demolished the last lingering traces of their lollypops.

"It's a jolly good house," said William.

"It ought to be for all that money," said Ginger bitterly. "Gosh! Five shillings jus' for a house!"

"Well, come on. Let's go in," said William. He was assailed by faint qualms as he stepped over the threshold but repressed them resolutely. "Well, we've *bought* it, haven't we?" he added as if refuting an unspoken argument.

They entered a roomy, well-furnished hall and made their way down a passage into a kitchen.

"Gosh!" said Douglas, who had opened a door that

led to the larder. "Look at all this stuff. A huge plate full of jam tarts. . . . D'you think we could have one?"

"'Course we can," said William. "Well, we've *bought* the place, haven't we? They're ours. Well,"— with his short ironic laugh—"it's news to *me* that you can buy a place an' then have it not b'longin' to you."

Ginger was inspecting his property a little morosely.

"There's a crack in that window," he said. "I've a good mind to go after her an' get sixpence back."

"Come on, Ginger," called William in a muffled voice from the larder. "There's jam tarts here an' sausage rolls an' some sardines an' a bit of pudding an' half a jelly. Gosh! It's a jolly good feast."

Ginger abandoned his grievances and joined the others in the larder. For some minutes there was silence, broken only by the sound of zestful munching.

"Well, we've not left much," said Henry at last.

"Why should we?" said William a little aggressively. "We're only eatin' our own food. We've *bought* it, haven't we?"

"What about this Houses of Parliament game?" said Ginger.

"Oh, yes," said William, putting the last of the cold pudding into his mouth. "Come on. Let's fix that up."

They trooped into the sitting-room, where William stood casting critical glances around him.

"I've always wanted a house of my own," he said. "I'm not goin' to have any carpets on the floor. I've never seen any sense in carpets. I like our house best when they're doin' the spring cleanin' an' you can make a smashin' noise goin' up an' down stairs an' walkin' about the floors without any carpets on 'em. . . . An' I'm not goin' to have all this furniture about. There isn't any sense in furniture, either. It only gets in your way when you're playin' games."

"You want a chair to sit on," said Douglas.

"No, you don't. You can sit on the floor. I think curtains are silly, too. There's no sense in curtains. They get in your way when you're climbin' in an' out of windows. I'm not goin' to have any curtains or furniture or carpets. I'm——"

"Yes, an' whose house is it?" interrupted Ginger indignantly. "Whose money bought it? I might have had"—he wrestled with a staggering sum in mental arithmetic and finally gave it up—"two rock lollypops a day for *years*, prob'ly, if I hadn't gone an' bought a house. I don't think it's much of one, either," he added gloomily. "It's not got any window you can get out on to the roof by. I've been up to look. I once stayed in a house that had a window right *in* the roof. It was wizard. I bet this house isn't worth more'n three an' six."

"Well, never mind," said William pacifically. "It'll make a good Houses of Parliament. Let's get on with the game." He turned to Henry. "What did you say those people in the Houses of Parliament were?"

"There's a Prime Minister," said Henry, "an' those others I said. The Whip an' the Black Rod. . . . Oh, an' there's a Foreign Secret'ry, too."

"I'll be the Prime Minister an' the Black Rod," said William.

"You jolly well won't," said Ginger. "You can't be two of them."

"Who says I can't?"

"I do," said Ginger.

A spirited scuffle, in which the other two joined, ranged over the sitting-room, upsetting a small table and sending the contents of the coal-scuttle over the hearth-rug, then drifted into the dining-room, where the four of them became entangled in a chenille curtain, bringing down the curtain, rod and all, on top of them. They disentangled themselves and rose, exhilarated and refreshed.

"All right," said William breathlessly. "I'll be Prime Minister an' you can be the rest."

"I'll be the Foreign Secret'ry," said Douglas. "I'm jolly good at bein' foreign." He extended his mouth in an imbecile grin, gesticulated wildly and said in a high-pitched squeaky voice, "Je suis, tu es, il est . . . hic, haec, hoc . . . bonus, bona, bonum . . . la plume, la porte, la fiddlededee, la thingamagig."

William and Ginger laughed hilariously, but Henry looked doubtful.

"I don't think the Foreign Secret'ry axshully *is* foreign," he said.

"'Course he is," said Douglas, elated by his success. "If he's called a foreign secret'ry he *mus'* be foreign."

"'Course he mus'," said William. "Stands to reason he mus'. Well, it's news to *me* if a foreign secret'ry isn't foreign. Why do they call him foreign if he isn't?"

"I think he's called foreign because he does foreign things," said Henry.

"No, he isn't," said Douglas. "He's called foreign because he *is* foreign. Anyway, I'm goin' to be him an' I'm goin' to be foreign. I know a lot more foreign words, too. I bet I could talk foreign for hours on end. Et tu, Brute . . . pommes de terre."

"All right, you can be Foreign Secret'ry," said William. "I think you'll make a jolly good one. Now what about the others?"

"I'll be the Whip," said Ginger, "an' Henry can be the chucker-out."

"The Black Rod," corrected Henry.

"All right . . . Well, come on. Let's look for a whip."

They raided the hatstand and the cupboard beneath the stairs, tossing the contents of the latter into the hall and overturning the former in an attempt to reach a native spear that was fastened to the wall high out of their reach. William finally secured it by climbing up the pegs of the hatstand, remaining miraculously unhurt when the whole thing collapsed on him. The blade had come loose from the wooden handle of the spear, and William, arising from the wreckage, tossed the blade carelessly on one side and examined the handle critically.

"Yes, it'll make a jolly good chucker-out thing," he said.

"All right. Give it me," said Henry.

"Mensa, mensare, mensavi, mensatum," said Douglas.

Henry took the spear handle and brandished it above his head with a flourish that brought a dinner gong to the ground with a resounding clatter.

"I'll have this, too," he said, seizing it and beating it with its small "drum stick."

"No, the Prime Minister's got to have that," said William. "He can bang it when he wants them to stop talking and listen to him."

While they were struggling for possession of the dinner-gong, Ginger, who had gone on a voyage of discovery, came leaping downstairs, waving a fishing rod above his head.

"Look what I've found for a whip," he said exultantly.

The hall became a bedlam of whip, spear-handle and gong. . . .

"If I'm goin' to be Foreign Secret'ry," said Douglas, raising his voice above the uproar, "I'm goin' to dress up foreign."

"Yes, that's a jolly good idea," said William. "Let's all dress up."

They plunged over the house, opening cupboards and drawers. The result was certainly impressive. William wore a tea cosy and a rain coat, Ginger a vegetable sieve and a pyjama jacket, Henry a tweed fishing hat and a trailing house-coat of flowered chintz. But the greatest sensation was provided by Douglas, who came slowly downstairs after the others had assembled in the hall, wrapped in a sheet, a pillow-case swathed round his head for a turban, his face thickly plastered with boot blacking.

"Gosh, Douglas, that's *jolly* fine!" said William.

"Monkety, flonkety, blonkety, plonkety," said Douglas, who had by now exhausted his limited store of French and Latin words.

"Well, come on. Let's start," said William.

"What'll we do first?" said Ginger.

"You an' Henry try an' chuck out me an' Douglas," said William. "That'll be the Whip an' the Black Rod tryin' to chuck out the Prime Minister an' the Foreign Secret'ry. Come on!"

"YOU—YOU ACTUALLY LIVE HERE?" SAID THE STOUT
WOMAN, HER EYES TAKING IN THE CHAOS ALL AROUND HER.

The struggle spread over the whole house, taking the final form of a sort of siege in which William and Douglas held their positions at the top of the stairs and Henry and Ginger tried to dislodge them. The four combatants fell down the stairs together and rolled into the hall.

"That was a jolly good fight," said William as he picked himself up.

"They call it a debate," said Henry.

"Well, it was a jolly good debate, then," said William. "Let's have another."

It was just as they were flinging themselves with renewed vigour into the second "debate" that there came the sound of two loud knocks at the front door. Sudden silence fell.

"Gosh!" said William.

He adjusted his tea-cosy, assumed an air of dignity and opened the front door.

A car was drawn up at the gate and at the front door stood a woman. She was very stout, but there was about her none of the good humour that is traditionally associated with stoutness. Her flabby face was set in lines of irritability, her small pig-like eyes gleamed with malice as they fell on William and the three curiously-garbed boys clustered behind him. She thrust them aside and stepped into the hall.

"What are you boys doing here?" she said.

"What d'you mean, what are we doin' here?" said William aggressively. "We live here. It's our house."

The woman sat down abruptly on a chair, the only piece of furniture in the hall that had escaped demolition.

"You—you actually *live* here?" she said.

"Yes," said William.

Her eyes took in the chaos of the hall—the over-turned hatstand and the piles of cushions, rugs, and deck-chairs, thrown out from the cupboard beneath the stairs. She went into the dining-room and saw the curtain dislodged from its rod, the hearthrug rucked up . . . went into the sitting-room and saw the overturned table and the coal scattered over the floor. She said nothing, but her small tight mouth became smaller and tighter, her flabby cheeks took on a purplish tinge. She sat down at the writing-table, wrote a note, put it into an envelope, brought it into the hall, laid it on the chair, then, darting a glance of fury at the four wondering boys, went out, slamming the door behind her.

"Crumbs!" said William.

"Well, she's gone, anyway," said Henry.

"Good riddance!" said Douglas, forgetting his rôle. Ginger had run upstairs and was looking out of a bedroom window.

"It's all right," he called. "She's got into the car an' she's drivin' off fast as she can. . . . She's gone right away now."

"Wonder who she was," said Henry.

"P'raps she was a lady burglar," suggested Douglas.

"Don't be such a chump," said Henry. "Burglars don't knock at doors."

"Yes, they do," said Douglas. "They knock to see if anyone's in."

"An' she looked at us to see if she could overpower us," said William. "An' when she saw she couldn't she went off."

"We could get her put in prison for that, you know,"
said Henry judicially. "Trespassin' on our property.
There's lors about it."

"Well, come on!" said William. "Let's start the
next fight—I mean debate. Let's have Henry an'
Douglas on the stairs an'——"

"William!" called Ginger from upstairs.

"Yes?"

"There's your mother an' a woman comin' down the
road."

"Oh . . ." said William. A stricken look came into
his face as he gazed at the devastation around him,
and a cold blast of reality invaded the roseate atmosphere of the Houses of Parliament. "P'r'aps it's time
we went home now. I mean, they mightn't understand
about us buyin' the house."

"We can't," said Ginger. "They've got so near
they'd see us if we went out."

"Well"—William gave another hunted look around
him—"p'r'aps we'd better try 'an clear up a bit. It's
got in a bit of a mess."

"They're comin' in at the gate, William, both of
them."

"Gosh!" said William. "Come on upstairs quick!"

The three Outlaws fled upstairs to join Ginger at the
bedroom window.

"If the worst comes to the worst," said William,
"we can climb out on to that balcony thing and get
on one of the branches of that tree an' climb down
into the garden an' get away that way."

"Y-yes," said Douglas doubtfully, "but it doesn't
look a very *safe* sort of tree to me."

.   .   .   .   .

Mrs. Brown and Mrs. Gilbert had met in the village shop.

"There doesn't seem to be any suet anywhere, does there?" said Mrs. Gilbert, packing her purchases into a bag and a basket. "I can't think what happens to it. I always thought it was an essential part of the animal."

"Perhaps animals are entering a new stage of evolution and being born without it," suggested Mrs. Brown.

They went out of the shop and began to walk along the road together.

"I tried that idea of giving the house to Patsy this morning," said Mrs. Gilbert. "I had to dash out to the shops and leave her in charge, in case the laundry came, so I said, 'Now I'm *giving* you the house while I'm away. It can be your own house.' She was so pleased and interested. I think it was an excellent idea."

"Yes," said Mrs. Brown, "I tried the one about the Houses of Parliament on William, too. I said, 'Collect your friends and have a sort of Houses of Parliament and discuss politics,' and he really seemed quite interested. Well"—she gave a laugh in which there was again that faint undertone of misgiving—"it ought to keep them out of mischief for *one* day at any rate. . . . Let me take your basket. You're very heavily laden."

"I am indeed," said Mrs. Gilbert, a shadow falling over her good-natured face. "I heard by this morning's post that Cousin Gertrude's coming to stay with us, so I just dashed out to get what I could. It's— it's a nightmare."

"Why is it a nightmare?" asked Mrs. Brown.

"Well, she's a sort of cousin," said Mrs. Gilbert, "and she just *comes*. She has no home of her own and she inflicts herself on various members of the family for months on end. I'm afraid I'm landed with her for the rest of the year. If my husband had been at home he might have headed her off; but he's abroad on business, and once she's in the place nothing can shift her."

"How very trying!" said Mrs. Brown sympathetically.

"It's more than trying," said Mrs. Gilbert. "She doesn't give you a chance of saying 'no'—not that I'm much good at saying 'no' anyway. She just sends a post card and *comes*. I'd so looked forward to a quiet time once I'd settled in the new house and, before I've been in it a fortnight, here she is! It wouldn't matter if she were different, but she's bad-tempered and irritable and—my dear, how she *eats*! As I said, it's just a nightmare."

"If I can help in any way . . ." said Mrs. Brown.

"That's very nice of you but no one can help," said Mrs. Gilbert. "It just has to be endured." They had reached the house with the elm tree in the garden. "You've never seen my new house. Do come in and have a look at it."

"I'd love to," said Mrs. Brown.

They opened the gate and began to walk up the little path.

"It's delightful," said Mrs. Brown, glancing over house and garden. "It looks so peaceful."

"It's too big for us, of course," said Mrs. Gilbert. "We may be letting off part of it when we've really settled in . . . but it's very charming."

She opened the front door.

"Patsy!" she called, then stopped short, gazing aghast at the overturned hatstand, and the cushions, rugs and deck-chairs strewn everywhere.

"Good Heavens!" she gasped. "What on earth's happened?"

"It must be burglars," said Mrs. Brown. "We had them once. They toss everything about everywhere just like that."

Mrs. Gilbert went into the dining-room, where curtain and curtain rod still lay collapsed on the floor.

"It can't be burglars," she said. "Everything's in a terrible muddle, but the silver's still on the sideboard. . . . Patsy!" she called again. "Oh, dear! What *can* have happened to her? I'm so worried."

Then she came back to the hall, saw the note on the chair, opened it and read aloud.

"DEAR ALICE,

"When you said that you were contemplating letting part of your house, I had no idea that you contemplated letting it to such a family of hooligans as appear to be in possession of it. A visit in such circumstances is an *impossibility*, and I am going straight on to Cousin Cecil's.

"Your cousin,

"GERTRUDE."

"Oh, what a *relief*!" she said. "But I do wish I knew where Patsy was."

Suddenly a curious figure appeared at the gate . . . Patsy had followed the Outlaws' instructions. She had circumvented the pond, with only a partial immersion.

She had scrambled through the hedge. She had found her way to the Marleigh sweet shop. She was sodden with mud, scratched, bedraggled, festooned with lollypops. Her face shone jubilantly beneath a coating of mire and "rock". She held four lollypops in each hand and four more protruded from each blazer pocket. Licking her lollypops, beaming delightedly, she approached her parent.

"*Patsy!*" screamed Mrs. Gilbert.

At that moment there came a cracking sound like a pistol shot, and a towsled, dishevelled form, its head enveloped in a tea-cosy, hurtled down from the tree, clutching the air wildly, and rolled to Mrs. Brown's feet.

"*William!*" screamed Mrs. Brown.

It was the next day. Mrs. Brown had gone round to see Mrs. Gilbert and met her coming out of her gate. The two stood there talking.

"His father was furious with him," said Mrs. Brown, "and of course we want to make good all the damage that was done."

"There really wasn't much," said Mrs. Gilbert. "Things were just knocked over. Nothing was broken. I've put back the curtains and the laundry will easily get the black off the pillow-case and sheet. . . . As to the food!" She laughed. "I'd bought in so lavishly for Cousin Gertrude that I was glad to see the larder cleared out. And—oh, my dear, the *relief* of not having her parked on me for months! It's worth every bit of it."

"Still, it was *dreadful*."

"It was Patsy's fault."

"Nonsense! It was William's."

At that moment Mrs. Monks, the President of the Women's Institute, appeared round the bend of the road and bore down upon them.

"Just the people I wanted to see," she said. "Mrs. Smith, who gave that very interesting lecture on Child Management last week, has written to say that she's willing to give a further lecture on the same subject. What do you think? Shall I ask her to or not?"

Mrs. Brown turned pale and Mrs. Gilbert clutched the gate-post for support.

"*Not !*" they moaned in unison.

CHAPTER III

WILLIAM AND THE AMERICAN TIE

"WELL, what'll we do now?" said Ginger. "We've done about everything you can do in a garden."

"An' some of the things you can't," said William with a certain modest pride.

The two sat on the roof of the tool-shed, surveying the garden beneath them. Rows of sagging runner beans bore witness to their journeys through the jungle as Red Indians, the herbaceous border showed traces of their forced landings as pilots from the branches of the copper beech that stretched above it, several stones had been dislodged from the rockery during their spirited attack and defence of a mountain fortress and the roller, after a short and inglorious career as a tank, had come to rest in the middle of the asparagus bed.

"Yes," added William thoughtfully, "p'r'aps we'd better go an' play somewhere else for a bit. I didn't re'lise that it—*showed* as much as what it does."

"P'r'aps it's 'cause we're lookin' at it from up here," said Ginger optimistically.

"Yes," said William, reassured by the explanation, "p'r'aps when you look at it flat it doesn't look so bad. Anyway, let's get away for a bit an' give people time to find it an' forget about it before they see us again."

"Let's go an' make a camp fire somewhere," said Ginger. "I've got some matches."

"No," said William. "Let's go to the wood an' try climbin' that tree again."

"All right," said Ginger, beginning to slither down the side of the tool-shed, "an' I bet we get to the top this time."

William let go his hold on the roof and rolled down to the ground, landing in the middle of a heap of potting soil that his father had carefully placed there the evening before. He stood up, brushing the soil from his person in a sketchy fashion.

"I bet we could make a sort of house in that tree if we got to the top," he said. "I'd like to go back to the days when people lived in trees. I think it ought to come back into fashion. People grumble 'cause they can't get houses, but they never seem to think of goin' back to trees. I bet trees 'd be much more fun to live in than houses."

"It'd be jolly difficult gettin' the furniture up," said Ginger. "Sideboards an' pianos an' baths an' things —an' I bet they'd always be tumblin' out of them. It'd be jolly difficult to balance them on the branches."

"We wouldn't need furniture, you chump," said William. "We'd jus' live in the branches same as the tree dwellers did. I bet if we all went back to bein' tree dwellers, we'd have a much jollier time than what we have now. We could graft apples an' gooseberries an' pears an' peaches an' grapes an' bananas an' pine-apples on the trees for food an' jus' eat 'em when we felt like it 'stead of havin' to come in for meals. I'd be a jolly good grafter but my father never lets me get any practice."

"Gosh, yes!" said Ginger as the possibilities of the idea opened out before him. "An' we wouldn't have to do any homework 'cause there wouldn't be any tables or ink."

"An' we could stay up as long as we liked," said William, "'cause there wouldn't be any beds an' we needn't go to school 'cause I don't expect ole Fathead can climb trees."

"Ole Fathead" was Mr. Vastop—a master who had joined the staff of William's school for a term to replace Mr. French, William's form master, while Mr. French took a much needed holiday to recover from an operation (and, incidentally, from William). Between William and Mr. French a feud had existed ever since their first meeting, but it was a feud run on established and almost friendly lines. They respected each other as foes and called an occasional truce in order to rally their forces and prepare for the next onslaught. But Mr. Vastop (inevitably nicknamed Old Fathead) was different. He was a rat-like little man with a long, thin nose and a small, pursed mouth that showed sharply projecting teeth. He was bad-tempered and sarcastic and had an unpleasant habit of luring his victims by friendly overtures to make confidences that he could use as weapons against them when opportunity arose. He had even—smiling his rat-like smile—drawn from William confidences about his beloved mongrel Jumble, only to comment in public on William's likeness to his "ill-conditioned cur" when next William arrived at school in his usual state of dishevelment.

"Oh, let's not think about *him*," said William. "He's not fit to live in a tree. A bog or a—a quicksand's where *he* ought to be. Anyway, it was sucks to him on Wednesday. Fancy thinkin' that Denis Compton played for Kent!"

"GOSH!" EXCLAIMED WILLIAM, PUTTING HIS HEAD
THROUGH THE WINDOW.

Last Wednesday William had passed Mr. Vastop holding forth with a knowledgeable air to a group of small boys and had corrected one of Mr. Vastop's statements as he passed with perhaps unnecessary brusqueness. Mr. Vastop's rat-like face had reddened, but William had vanished before he could think of an adequate rejoinder.

"He's jus' ign'rant," continued William contemptuously. "What's the use of him havin' all those letters after his name if he thinks that Denis Compton plays for Kent? He's the mos' ign'rant man I've ever met."

"Well, never mind him," said Ginger. "Let's get on with this tree house."

They skirted the side of the house and passed the open sitting-room window. Through the open window they had an unimpeded view of Robert and a girl with eyes of periwinkle blue sitting side by side on the settee. The girl was just handing Robert what appeared to be a tie of virulent colour and design.

"Gosh!" said William, putting his head in at the window in order to inspect the strange object at closer quarters.

"Get out!" thundered Robert.

William got out.

"Who is she?" said Ginger as they proceeded on their way.

"She's that girl that the family of's come to live at The Cedars," said William. "She's just got back from staying with some relations in America an' she's called some awful name I can't remember—something like rock cakes but a bit diff'rent—an' Robert says she's the mos' beautiful girl he's ever seen."

"She looked jolly ordin'ry to me," said Ginger.

"They all look jolly ordin'ry," said William, "but"— with rising excitement—"did you see that tie she was givin' him? I've never seen a tie like that before. It'd got people an' balls an' things all over it."

"Oh, never mind it," said Ginger. "Come on to the woods an' let's get goin' with the tree house."

In the sitting-room Robert winced and blenched as Roxana held the tie before his eyes.

"They're all the rage in New York," she said. "They're so much smarter than the dull ties people wear in England, aren't they?"

"Yes," said Robert, rallying his shattered forces.

"I chose it specially for you, Robert. I wanted to bring you something that would—well, that would be a sort of symbol of the bond between us. I wanted it to *mean* something. I'm funny like that, you know, Robert. I like things to *mean* something."

"Yes," agreed Robert, trying to hide his bewilderment. "Yes—er—quite."

"You see, it's modern," said Roxana earnestly. "It isn't stuffy and old-fashioned like spots and stripes and things. It belongs to the new world that you and I belong to—the world that isn't bound by the old conventions and ideas. I'm funny like that, you know, Robert. I can't bear old conventions and ideas. What I'm trying to say, Robert, is that it's more than just a tie."

Robert gazed at the stalwart, strangely accoutred figures of baseball players who, in various attitudes— springing, crouching, leaping, grovelling—adorned the strip of material. A ball appeared at intervals but without much indication as to what part it played in the nightmare gambol.

"Yes," said Robert, feeling himself on firmer ground. "Yes, I can see that it is."

"It's almost what one might call a *gage d' amour*, Robert." She threw him a melting glance from the periwinkle blue eyes. "You understand what that means, don't you?"

"Well," Robert gave a short nervous laugh and passed his hand along the inside of his collar. Roxana's French had been superbly Parisian and Robert's, like that of Chaucer's nun, belonged to the school of Stratford-atte-Bowe. "Well—er——"

"French, you know," said Roxana kindly.

"Oh, yes, that!" said Robert in a tone of relief. "Yes . . . I can't say it like you do"—reverently—"but I know what you mean now.   It—it's wonderful of you, Roxana."

"It's a sort of *token*, Robert, that we share the same ideals, that the same things *mean* the same things to us, that we both want to throw overboard everything that's old-fashioned and out-of-date and—insular."

Robert looked at the tie again.   It was growing on him.   No one else in the village had anything to compare with it.   It would, he felt, confer a certain distinction on him, raise him above the ruck of people who wore small spots and stripes round their collars. Already he heard himself saying in a tone of airy amusement:

"Haven't you really seen one like this before?   Oh, everyone wears them in New York."

"I'll put it on now, shall I?" he said, beginning to undo the sober length of navy and white rayon that enclosed his neck.

Roxana laid a hand on his arm.

"No, Robert.   I want to make a sort of *occasion* of it.   I'm funny like that, you know.   When a thing means a lot to me I like to make a sort of *occasion* of it. You see, I'm having a party on Thursday for my friends—my own special friends—and I want you to come to it.   And—perhaps it sounds silly but I'm funny like that—I want you to wear the tie then for the first time.   If you come to the party wearing the tie it will be a sign that we're *real* friends, that you feel the same as I do about stuffiness and convention and that sort of thing.   And if you don't——"

"But, Roxana, of course I do," said Robert earnestly. "Of course I'll wear the tie."

"Think it over, Robert. Think it over carefully. It means such a lot to both of us," said Roxana in a tone of deep solemnity. "Only last year——"

She stopped and her face darkened as at some painful memory.

"Yes, dear?" encouraged Robert.

"There was a man . . . He *seemed* to share all my ideas about that sort of thing and I went out to New York to stay with my cousins just as I did this year —and I brought back a tie for him, just as I have done for you. It was like this but perhaps a little more daring"—Robert looked at the tie and blinked—"and I said to him just what I've said to you and told him to wear it at my party if he really felt for me what he said he felt for me and—and——"

"Yes?"

"He just didn't. He pretended he'd lost it. Did you ever hear of such a cowardly trick? He just didn't wear it and said he'd lost it. I never spoke to him again. I never looked at him again. He didn't *mean* anything any more. I'm funny like that, you know. Once a person lets me down they never mean anything to me any more."

"But of course I'll wear the tie at your party, Roxana," said Robert. "It's wonderful of you to ask me."

"It was such a *cowardly* excuse to say he'd lost it, wasn't it? I saw him then as he really was. I cut him right out of my life. You think I was right, don't you, Robert?"

"Indeed I do." said Robert fervently.

c

"And you won't wear it *before* the party, will you?"

"Of course not," said Robert. "As a matter of fact I couldn't wear it before because I'm going off on a few days' hiking holiday with Jameson tomorrow, and I shan't be back till Thursday afternoon, anyway."

Roxana heaved a long, deep sigh.

"I'm afraid I'm a rather complicated and unusual character, Robert," she said. "Not many people really understand me. That's the great tragedy of my life. I have very high ideals for my friends and so few of them come up to them. . . . I expect you think I'm very foolish, don't you, Robert?"

"I think you're adorable," said Robert, glad to have reached a point where he felt sure of his ground. "I think that everything about you's adorable—your eyes, your hair, your mouth and—well, I love your name, too. Roxana. . . . It's the most beautiful name I've ever heard in my life."

"Well, it's *me*, isn't it?" said Roxana. "As soon as I saw it—in some book, I've forgotten which—I knew it was me. My parents had me christened Elsie. I've tried to forgive them for it, but it hasn't been easy. I feel things so deeply. Elsie!" She shuddered. "It just isn't me at all, and if a thing isn't me I just can't put up with it. It seems to cramp my whole personality. I'm funny like that, Robert . . . I was a little tempted by Perdita at one time, but as soon as I saw Roxana I knew it was me."

"Roxana . . ." repeated Robert, lingering bemusedly over the syllables. "It's the most beautiful name I've ever heard in my life, and it suits you so."

"Well, it does show that I'm just a little out of the ordinary, doesn't it?"

"Out of the ordinary?" repeated Robert ardently. "Oh, Roxana, when first I saw you . . ."

The conversation continued on familiar lines.

The building of the house in the tree also continued on familiar lines.

William fell out of his tree and tore his shirt, got soaked to the skin in an effort to "lay on" water from the stream to his improvised "bedroom", lost both handkerchief and garters during the process of turning the top branch into a flag staff, acquired a coating of soot in an attempt to build a fire in the "sitting-room" . . . and at last was chased from the wood—with Ginger close at his heels—by an infuriated keeper whose threats of vengeance added the final touch of colour to an already colourful morning.

"Gosh!" panted William when they had reached the safety of the main road. "He said some jolly int'restin' things this time, didn't he?"

"Yes," said Ginger. "He's thought out some fresh ones since las' time. . . . You know, I dunno that trees are all that good as houses."

"Well, let's try a diff'rent sort nex' time," said William. "I bet that big fir tree would be better. Once you get started on fir trees they're jolly easy to climb."

"But there's not much room on the branches," said Ginger. "I bet that oak would be better."

"We'll try 'em both," said William, "an' we'll have to make a sort of lift for Jumble to get up it. I've tried to teach him to climb trees but he can't. He gets all muddled up with his legs."

"We could tie a rope round his middle an' jus' pull him up."

"Yes," agreed William but he spoke absently.

His thoughts were not with the tree house. They were with the tie that he had seen Roxana present to Robert.

"Gosh, wasn't it wizard!" he said. "Men playin' football all over it. I've never seen one like that before. Gosh! A *tie* with men playin' football all over it!"

"I didn't see it prop'ly," said Ginger, "but if it's American it mus' be baseball, not football."

"Well, baseball, then," said William. "I'll show it you if I get a chance. I know where he keeps his ties."

He described it to Henry and Douglas. He described it to the whole form. He found himself committed— before he quite realised it—to bringing the tie to school and displaying it at "break" the next day. He felt certain qualms about the undertaking, but Robert's absence on his hiking holiday seemed to make the risk comparatively negligible. I'll jus' take it there an' bring it back, he assured himself. If I jus' take it there an' bring it back, nothin' can happen to it. . . .

Cautiously, warily, he entered Robert's bedroom and opened the wardrobe door. There, on a string stretched across the back of the door, hung Robert's ties . . . but the new one was not among them. Robert had heard his mother casually mention a Jumble Sale that was to be held at the Women's Institute on the Saturday of his absence and, remembering the last occasion of a Women's Institute Jumble Sale, to which she had contributed an assortment of his most cherished possessions, he had found, as he thought, a safe and secret hiding-place for the precious tie at the bottom

"GIVE THAT TO ME, BROWN," SAID MR. VASTOP.

of a box of collars in the top drawer of his chest of drawers. And there, after an unsystematic but thorough search, William found it, still wrapped in tissue paper, carefully concealed in the cardboard box beneath the circle of collars.

He slipped it into his pocket and set off for school, where his highest expectations were fulfilled. His contemporaries crowded round him at "break", spellbound by the gaudiness and vigour of his exhibit. Rising to the occasion, William gave a spirited account of the game of baseball, invented on the spur of the moment.

"This one's tryin' to jump over that one an' this one's crawling along to get nearer the goal post an' this one's doin' a native war dance—it's part of the game—an' this one's——"

"Gosh! What a lot of balls!" said someone.

William hastily counted them.

"Yes, they play with seven balls," he said. "It's part of the game."

The crowd gave a gasp of wonder and amazement.

"Oh, yes," said William, who was by this time carried a little beyond himself. "Seven balls is nothin' to them. You can play with as many balls as you like in baseball. You try an' hit one ball with another ball, same as you do in billiards . . ."

He realised that he was getting a little out of his depth and was relieved when, at this point, the bell rang and his audience swarmed indoors. But the whole thing had gone to his head. He had enjoyed holding forth to a spellbound audience as a baseball authority and he wanted to go on doing it. Several other imaginary features of the game had occurred to him. He nudged Frankie Parker, who sat at the next desk, and took the tie from his pocket again.

"Look, Frankie," he whispered. "This one with his mouth open's the captain an' he's doin' the native war cry. It goes like this——"

The sharp thin hand of Mr. Vastop descended on his shoulder, and the sharp thin voice of Mr. Vastop cut into the first whispered notes of the war cry.

"Give that to me, Brown."

And Mr. Vastop strode back to his desk, bearing the captured tie with an air of triumph.

"Our friend Brown has a somewhat flashy taste in ties," he said, holding it at arm's-length and inspecting it with his rat-like sneer. "A taste that should not be encouraged in one so young. A good thing, perhaps, that he will not now have the opportunity of disporting himself in this particular specimen."

The lid of Mr. Vastop's desk closed over the tie and horror closed over William. He did not know about Roxana's party and Robert's solemn undertaking to wear the tie for that occasion, but he knew that the tie was a present to Robert from Roxana, he knew that his inspection of the tie through the open window had betrayed his interest in it, he knew that Robert would instantly connect its disappearance with that interest . . . and he knew that retribution at the hands of Robert would be swift and sure.

"It's all right," he assured his friends after class with a confidence he did not feel. "I'll tell him it's Robert's. He'll let me have it back all right if I tell him it's Robert's. I—I'll jus' have a word with him at the end of school."

"I bet he'll be mad," said Ginger, "an' I bet he'll say you can't have it back till the end of term."

William's friends watched William having a word with Mr. Vastop at the end of school. Mr. Vastop was not mad. Mr. Vastop was, on the contrary, delighted. Mr. Vastop considered that William had "shown him up" in the matter of the cricketer and he never forgave anyone who showed him up. He welcomed the opportunity of getting even with William and intended to make full use of it.

William's usually ruddy countenance had paled a little by the time he rejoined his friends.

"Gosh!" he said. "He says he's not goin' to give it me back at all. I told him it was Robert's an' he didn't care. I told him I'd get in an awful row with Robert an' he didn't care about that either. I told

him Robert'd be mad with him an'—gosh!—he didn't
even seem to care about that. I said he could do
anythin' he liked to me—he could *torcher* me if he
liked—if only he'd let me have it back. I said he
could pull my teeth out an' screw my thumbs same as
they used to do to people in hist'ry."

"An' what did he say to that?" said Ginger.

"He said that mental torture was much more
effective an' that he'd enjoy watchin' me undergo it
an' that he hoped Robert would apply the other sort
of torture to me . . . an' I bet he will, too!"

"Well, there isn't anythin' you can do about it, is
there?" said Ginger.

William frowned thoughtfully.

"There's nearly a week before Robert comes back.
I might try somethin' . . ."

"What can you try?"

"I'll try meltin' his heart first," said William after
a slight pause. "He's a villain all right, but lots of
villains get their hearts melted in books an' I don't see
why he shouldn't get his melted. Even a villain's
got a better self an' I'm jolly well goin' to try 'n' find
his."

But William's search was unrewarded. He produced
a geography exercise that, except for a few blots and
several wild misstatements, was as perfect as he could
well make it. He spent a whole evening learning
history dates, which he repeated, with only a pardonable degree of inaccuracy, the next day. He picked up
a pencil that Mr. Vastop had dropped and presented
it to him, teeth bared in a polite smile. He even,
when Mr. Vastop joined the spectators of the Saturday
afternoon cricket match, moved forward a chair for

him, resisting a strong temptation to draw it back just as Mr. Vastop was sitting down . . . and Mr. Vastop received all these attentions with a rat-like smile that showed the deep pleasure he took in the situation. The days slipped by till Wednesday, the eve of Robert's return.

"Well, he's not got a better self," said William firmly. "I've tried to find one an' he jus' hasn't got one. He's one of those villains without a better self, same as Hitler an' Nero an' that man at the Income Tax my father's always talkin' about. I'll have to do somethin' desp'rate. With Robert comin' back tomorrow it'll *have* to be somethin' desp'rate."

"Gosh!" said Ginger. "You aren't goin' to kidnap him or anythin', are you?"

William considered the suggestion with interest and abandoned it reluctantly.

"N-no, I don't think so. It'd take too long to fix up an' I wouldn't know where to keep him an' there'd be an awful row about it when he came out."

"What're you goin' to do, then?" said Ginger.

"I'm goin' to get it back," said William. "He's taken it out of his desk 'cause I've looked, so it mus' be in his house. I'm goin' to wait till there's no one in his house, an' then I'm goin' to go in an' fetch it."

"Gosh! You could get put in prison for that," said Ginger.

"Well, I shouldn't mind goin' to prison as long as I'd got that tie back first. I don't s'pose they'd put me in prison straight away. I heard someone say that prisons are jolly full up nowadays, so I 'spect people have got to wait their turn same as they have to for hospitals. Anyway, if I was in prison I'd

miss his rotten ole hist'ry an' geography lessons. An'
I could always escape when I'd had enough of it.
I've always wanted to try escapin' from prison. I'd
saw through the bars an' let myself down by tyin' my
sheets together an' then I'd——"

It was clear that William was in danger of being
carried away by this theme, so Ginger hastily interrupted:

"Yes, but about that tie . . ."

"Oh, yes," said William, reluctantly tearing himself
from the mental contemplation of his daring escape
from prison and returning to the matter in hand.
"Yes, about the tie . . . Well, we'll go to his house,
same as I said, an' wait till he's gone out an'—well—
jus' go in an' take it. I bet he'll leave a window open.
People always do. An' if he doesn't I bet I can climb
up by that shed an' get in by an upstairs window,
same as I do for my mother when she forgets her
key."

"S'pose there's a charwoman or someone there?"

"There won't be. Ole Fathead's got ole Frenchie's
house an' ole Frenchie's charwoman, an' she only goes
there in the morning."

"When'll we do it?"

"Today, of course. It's a matter of life an' death.
If we don't do it today we're ru'ned. At least I am.
When Robert's mad he sticks at nothin'. . . . Let's
go home for tea an' then go round to ole Fathead's an'
do it."

Mr. Vastop, sallying forth from his house an hour
later, did not notice the two small boys who lurked
in the shadow of the hedge on the other side of the
road.

"Come on, quick!" said William, as the small dapper figure vanished from view. "There's a window open. I bet it won't take two minutes to get in an' find that tie an' get out again."

Luck seemed to be with them. The road was empty and remained empty as they raised the window sash and entered the little sitting-room of Mr. French's house, now in the temporary possession of Mr. Vastop.

"Ole Frenchie used to keep things he confiscated in this drawer," said William, opening a drawer in the bureau. "He's often given me things back out of it when I've pleaded with him. He's a villain, same as ole Fathead, but he's got a better self."

A thorough search of the drawer, however, revealed only neat stacks of notepaper and envelopes . . . boxes of paper clips . . . coloured pencils . . . a tin of throat lozenges . . . copies of Mr. Vastop's testimonials, which William read with incredulous surprise, and a photograph of Mr. Vastop himself, to which William could not resist adding a turned-up moustache, an enormous pipe and a feathered hat.

"S'not there," he said at last, slamming the drawer back into place. "Let's try that cupboard."

"You're makin' an awful noise, banging about," said Ginger. "I bet someone'll hear from the road an' come in to see what's happ'nin'."

William looked round the room.

"All right, let's turn the wireless on," he said. "I bet no one'll wonder what's happ'nin' if they hear the wireless on."

He switched on the knob and the strains of a military band filled the room.

"We mus' leave things tidy, too," said Ginger a

"YOU CERTAINLY SHOWED SOME PLUCK, SIR," SAID
THE POLICEMAN.

little nervously. "We'll get in an awful row if he
finds out we've been."

"All right," said William, carefully replacing a pile
of old magazines in the cupboard and resisting the
temptation to sample a tin of biscuits that reposed
beneath them. "Let's try that chest of drawers over
there now."

The search continued. The military band gave place
to a play that seemed to consist chiefly of a dialogue
between two men. The cupboard and chest of drawers
were explored without success. It was just as they
were on the point of reluctantly abandoning the search
that Ginger gave a gasp and said:

"He's comin' back, William. He's jus' openin' the gate."

"Gosh!" said William. "Let's hide quick!"

Ginger dived behind the cupboard, William behind a large arm-chair. From his hiding-place William saw Mr. Vastop enter the gate jauntily, then stop and grow pale as the voices of the radio dialogue (lowered at a dramatic point of the plot) reached him through the open window. He stood there, staring at the house, his rat-like mouth drawn into a grin of terror. Then he started back to the gate. Frankie Parker was passing along the road.

"Parker!" squeaked Mr. Vastop in a high-pitched agitated voice. "Run to the police station at once and tell them to send someone here quickly. Say that I've come back from the village to find burglars in the house. Hurry! Hurry! Hurry!"

"Yes, sir," said Frankie and set off at a decorous trot down the road. Nothing had ever been known to ruffle Frankie's composure.

As Mr. Vastop still stood gazing in fascinated horror at the house, the voices of the actors died away and the announcer's voice, clear and resonant, floated out to him.

"That was *Peril of Life*, a play by Adrian Ashtead. . . . The time is now half-past five. . . . We present Donald Macalastair's Dance Band. . . ."

There followed the lilting strains of a dance band.

Mr. Vastop's mouth dropped open to its fullest extent. His eyes goggled. . . . He ran to the front door, unlocked it and entered the sitting-room. There he stood, gazing at the wireless, his mouth opening and shutting distractedly.

"Oh, dear! Oh, dear!" he jibbered. "I must have left it on after tea. I quite thought I'd turned it off. Oh, dear! Oh, dear!"

He took out his handkerchief and mopped his brow. Then, as if coming to a sudden decision, he switched off the knob . . . opened the drawers of his bureau and tossed their contents on the floor . . . twisted his tie awry, rumpled his hair, pulled his shirt about . . . over-threw a small chair . . . kicked the hearthrug to one side . . . scattered a few objects from the chimneypiece on to the hearth and emptied the contents of a small bookcase over the carpet. He had just completed these preparations when the stalwart figure of the policeman appeared at the gate and made its majestic way up to the front door.

"Come in, Constable," called Mr. Vastop, panting noisily. "You're just too late. I dealt with the fellows as best I could, but I'm afraid they got away. Here's the battle-field."

He waved his hand in a sweeping gesture round the disordered room.

"Blimey!" said the policeman, surveying the scene and taking his note-book from his pocket. "Perhaps you'll tell me just what happened, sir?"

"Certainly, Constable, certainly," said Mr. Vastop. "I heard the fellows' voices and caught a glimpse of them through the window as I came in at the gate, so I sent a boy who was passing to fetch you and came in myself to do the best I could without you. I found two men here just turning out the contents of the bureau, as you see."

"Yes, sir. . . . Could you describe them, sir?"

"Certainly, Constable, certainly. . . . Both were

large men. One was dark, in a dark suit, and the other was—er—fair, in a light suit. I closed with them at once so naturally I hadn't time to notice many details."

"Of course, sir," said the policeman, writing busily.

"I knocked the first one down, but the other then closed with me, and, while I was dealing with him, the first one got up. I managed to get to the door and hoped to hold them till you came. I gave the fair one a blow that sent him reeling against the bookcase, knocking the books out, as you see, and then I had a struggle with both of them together in which I certainly didn't come off worst. I think"—he gave his short sarcastic laugh—"that you'll find one with a broken nose and the other with a dislocated jaw."

"You certainly showed some pluck, sir," said the policeman respectfully.

Mr. Vastop repeated his short sarcastic laugh.

"Oh, well . . . I may be lacking in many good qualities, but I flatter myself that I am not deficient in courage. . . . The two of them got away at last, however, and, I'm afraid, have made good their escape."

The policeman looked at the contents of the bureau, strewn about the room.

"Much missing, sir?" he said.

"Fortunately not," said Mr. Vastop. "Nothing missing, as a matter of fact. They hadn't really started on the job when I disturbed them—and I think that 'disturb' is the right word. Ha, ha!"

"You can't describe them more fully, sir?" said the policeman.

"Oh, yes, I think I can," said Mr. Vastop, whose

imagination had had time for a little exercise in the interval. "The dark one had a heavy moustache and—er—a bulbous nose . . . and the fair one was —er—going slightly bald over one temple with—er— with bulbous eyes. They were both villainous-looking men. Real gangster types."

"You've come out of it very well, sir," said the policeman. "I must say, I congratulate you on your courage. . . . Well, I'll get back with my report now. We *may* be able to catch them, but they've probably got clear into the woods by now and there's no telling what direction they'll take from there. Good-bye for the present, sir."

"Good-bye, Constable," said Mr. Vastop, showing his sharp projecting teeth in an effusive smile, "and I'll hold myself ready for further questioning, of course. Ha, ha!"

The policeman took his majestic departure and Mr. Vastop set to work, putting the room to rights. It was while he was picking up the ornaments from the hearth that he suddenly caught sight of William crouching behind the chair. He stared at him in horrified amazement. Once more his mouth dropped open and his eyes bulged.

"How dare you!" he spluttered. "How *dare* you! What do you mean by it!" His thin arm darted out and dragged William from his hiding-place. "What do you mean by trespassing in my private room! I'll —I'll——"

"I came 'cause I wanted that tie you took off me," said William simply.

"We've not done any harm," said Ginger, emerging from his hiding-place. "We've only looked for it."

"I shall report you both to the Headmaster," said Mr. Vastop. "I'll get you both expelled. I'll——" He stopped short and a thoughtful look came into his face. "How long have you been here?"

"All the time," said William. He spoke in a tone of guileless innocence. His face was devoid of expression. "We were here when you came in and turned the wireless off."

"We were here when you started upsetting the room," said Ginger.

"We were here when the policeman came," said William.

Mr. Vastop stood looking at them. An ashen hue had invaded his cheeks. His rats' teeth shot out in a ghastly smile.

"You probably completely misunderstood the situation, my boys," he said. "Completely misunderstood it. It was—it was——" His face was contorted with effort as he searched for an explanation . . . then inspiration came and his teeth shot out again. "It was a wager. Yes, that was it. A wager. A wager I'd had with a friend. He bet me that I couldn't get away with it and I bet him that I could. You understand, don't you, boys? Just a wager. A bet. A sort of joke. Ha, ha!"

"Yes," said William. His face was still a bland expressionless mask. "We'll 'splain that when we tell people about it, shall we?"

"No, no," said Mr. Vastop with a snarl that was evidently intended to be a conciliatory laugh. "Oh no, no, no! You mustn't tell anyone. It would be —it would be betraying my friend's confidence for you to tell anyone about it. I—I—I gave my friend my

"WE WERE HERE WHEN THE POLICEMAN CAME," SAID
WILLIAM.

word that no one should know about it. I depend
on your honour to say nothing of this to anyone."

William's face was now so expressionless that his
homely features might have been hacked out of wood.
He stared glassily in front of him.

"I've got a very bad mem'ry," he said. "It's a
funny thing but I've got a sort of feeling that if you
gave me back that tie of Robert's I wouldn't be able
to remember anything else. It'd drive everything else
clean out of my head."

Mr. Vastop's face darkened.

"I told you——" he began severely, then stopped.
"It's in my bedroom," he went on. "I'll get it."

He went from the room. William turned his expressionless face to Ginger and slowly lowered one eyelid.
Mr. Vastop returned, holding the tie, still wrapped in

tissue paper, in his hand.   He had recovered something
of his poise.

"As you appear to be sorry for your disgraceful be-
haviour," he said, "I am willing to overlook it this
once and let you have the—er—the confiscated article
back.   But I hope that this will be a lesson to
you."

"Yes, sir," said William woodenly.

"And I take it that you will—er—respect my friend's
confidence?"

"You mean, not tell anyone?" said William.   "No,
we won't tell anyone now we've got the tie back."

Mr. Vastop heaved a sigh of relief.   William, he
knew, had almost every other conceivable failing, but
he was not a boy who broke his word.   He handed
the tie back to William.   William slipped it into his
pocket, and the two boys set off down the road.   Mr.
Vastop, standing at the window to watch their departure, once more took out his handkerchief and mopped
his brow.

Cautiously, silently, William and Ginger made their
way up to Robert's bedroom and opened the drawer
where the collar box had been.   The collar box was no
longer there.

"Gosh!" said William.   "What's happened to it?"

"Never mind," said Ginger.   "Stick the thing anywhere and let's get away quick.   I'm sick of this ole
tie business.   I want to get back to tree climbing.   I
want to try that fir tree."

"All right," said William.   "I'll stick it here under
his handkerchiefs.   I bet he'll make a fuss about it
when he comes home, anyway."

And Robert did make a fuss about it when he came home.

Arriving barely in time to change for Roxana's party, he dashed upstairs, his face glowing with happy anticipation, then dashed downstairs, his face set in lines of horror.

"Mother, where's that box of collars that was in the top drawer of my chest of drawers?"

Mrs. Brown looked up placidly from her mending.

"I sent it to the Jumble Sale, dear," she said.

"You sent it——"

Robert's voice failed him.

"Yes, dear. It was the box of collars that Aunt Maggie sent you for Christmas last year, wasn't it, and you said that they were a size too large. I remember that you said they were a size too large and I don't believe in hoarding things one can't use. Better let someone else have the use of them."

"But underneath the collars in the box . . ." said Robert hoarsely. "Didn't you look underneath the collars in the box?"

"No, dear," said Mrs. Brown. "Why should I? I just sent the box as it was."

"Great Heavens!" said Robert wildly, as the full force of the tragedy struck him. "She'll never believe . . . she'll *never* believe . . ."

"Who'll never believe what, dear?" said Mrs. Brown, breaking off a length of thread and holding her needle up to the light.

Robert gave a bitter laugh.

"Well, I only hope you'll never know what you've done to me," he said. "I only hope——" He noticed William hovering in the doorway and turned on him savagely.   "Don't stand there listening to what doesn't concern you.   Clear off!"

"Have you looked under your handkerchiefs, Robert?" said William innocently.

"Have I——?" began Robert in a voice of thunder, then stopped suddenly and took the stairs three at a time.

In a few seconds he returned, carrying the tie. William and Ginger were just going out of the front door.

"Yes, it was there," said Robert.

"I thought it might be," said William.   "Come on, Ginger."

"Here! One minute!" said Robert, his mind a turmoil of relief, suspicion and bewilderment.

"'Fraid we've got to go," said William from the gate. "We want to make a tree house.   We've wasted a lot of time already."

Robert stared after them as they ran down the road, his mind wrestling with the inexplicable disappearance and reappearance of the tie.   He'd bet anything the little blighters knew something about it.   Now he came to think of it, everything in his drawer looked as if it had been messed about.   He hesitated, wondering whether to run after them and force the truth out of them; then decided to let things rest as they were. Where William was concerned it was often safer to let things rest as they were.   He'd got the tie back and that was all that mattered.   And there was no more time to be lost. . . .   Standing in front of the hall mirror, he fastened the lurid strip round his neck; then, a beatific smile on his face, set off briskly for Roxana's party.

CHAPTER IV

ARCHIE ON THE RUN

"FOOD!" said William, surveying the kitchen table with an air of aloof disapproval. "Grown-ups never seem to know when to stop eatin'."

"Now, William," said Mrs. Brown mildly, "it's only a little party for the Dramatic Society. They want to fix things up for this play that they're going to do."

"Thought they'd fixed 'em up," said William, appropriating a cheese straw, carrying it to his mouth and swallowing it in one swift movement. "They've had enough meetings. Talk an' eat—that's all they can do."

"Well, stop chattering and eating cheese straws, dear," said Mrs. Brown, taking a tray of pastry cases out of the oven. "Things crop up, you know. People turn out to be not suitable for their parts and—well, there's the scenery and things to be discussed."

"What are those?" said William, turning his frowning gaze on to the pastry cases.

"Pastry cases, dear. They're going to be filled with mushroom and white sauce mixture and things like that."

"If I eat this one it'll save you the trouble of fillin' it, won't it?" said William virtuously.

"*No*," said Mrs. Brown, too late to save the pastry case. "Now, William, do go away."

"I wouldn't mind bein' in this play they're gettin' up," said William in a voice muffled by the pastry case, "if they've got a part of someone steeped in crime. I can act someone steeped in crime jolly well. Or I wouldn't mind bein' the keen-eyed sloth——"

"You mean sleuth, William."

"Well, the one that dogs the footsteps of the one that's steeped in crime an' tracks him to his doom. I'm jolly good at actin' parts like that. I once wrote a play about a doughy hero——"

"You mean doughty, William, and come away from the larder door."

"Gosh!" said William, his voice hoarse with indignation. "Look at all that food. Sausage rolls an' jam tarts an' . . . Isn't this party of Ethel's ever goin' to *stop* eatin'?"

"Well, dear, they're having drinks and cheese straws and things when they arrive at about six and they're going to have a cold buffet with coffee later on at about nine. The things in the larder are for the cold buffet."

"Are you sure it's enough?" said William with heavy sarcasm. "I shouldn't like 'em to starve   P'raps they'd better have a hunch of ven'son as well an'—an' a few oxes roasted whole jus' to sort of fill up gaps."

"Now, William, don't be silly," said Mrs. Brown.

"When Ginger an' me got up a play"—William's figure had vanished into the larder and his voice seemed to come from a far distance—"I don't remember anyone makin' these c'lossal feasts for us. I don't remember anyone givin' us mountains of sausage rolls an' things. Well, it's news to *me* if they did . . ."

His voice had become more and more indistinct and now faded away altogether.

"William, leave those things alone," said Mrs. Brown, turning a harassed glance from the white sauce she was stirring over the cooker to the open larder door from which issued sounds suggestive of a boy munching pastry, "and come out of there."

William came out. His mouth was ringed with pastry crumbs and his face wore an expression of bland innocence.

"I've not eaten anythin'," he said. "Nothin' to speak of, anyway. I jus' cleared up one or two of those jam tarts that would have fallen off the dish soon as anyone moved it. An' one of those sausage rolls was the wrong shape so I thought I'd better eat that too, 'cause it didn't look right with the others."

"Oh, thank goodness! Here's Ethel," said Mrs. Brown.

Ethel entered the kitchen and put her shopping basket on the table.

"I think I've remembered everything," she said. "Salted nuts . . . potato crisps . . . celery . . . cream cheese . . . mayonnaise . . . Come away from those potato crisps, William."

"I was only lookin' at 'em," said William aggrievedly. "Gosh! Anyone'd think I was goin' to eat 'em!"

"Yes, anyone would," said Ethel shortly as she removed the bag from his reach.

"Did you bring the loaf, Ethel?" said Mrs. Brown. "We decided that we'd better have another to be on the safe side, you remember."

"Oh, bother! I forgot it," said Ethel.

A look of relief came into Mrs. Brown's face.

"William will fetch it, then, won't you, William?"

she said. "Here's the money and there's no hurry for it so you can take your time."

"All right," said William, pocketing the money. "Can I have a few sausage rolls jus' to eat on the way? It'll save you havin' a lot left over an' goin' bad."

"No," said Mrs. Brown and Ethel simultaneously.

"Oh, all right," said William. "I'll try not to eat the loaf, comin' back, but I've got awful gnawin' pains of hunger all over me."

"Don't be ridiculous, William," said Mrs. Brown. "Oh, well . . ." She handed him a couple of pastry cases. "Now off you go!"

Munching vigorously, he went down the garden path and vanished from sight.

"Good riddance!" said Ethel. "Now let's set to work on the sandwiches."

They sat at the table, cutting the sandwiches and enjoying the feeling of peace that William's departure generally left behind it.

"How many people exactly are you expecting this evening, dear?" said Mrs. Brown.

"Well, there are ten in the cast and one or two helpers. About thirteen, I should think . . . Where's the cheese grater? Has William eaten it?"

"No, dear. Here it is. Now tell me about the play. I've been so busy with one thing and another that I really know very little about it and I must be primed for the party. What's the plot of it?"

"Well, it's rather difficult to explain," said Ethel.

It was certainly difficult to explain . . . It had been written by Oswald Franks, the Secretary of the Dramatic Society, and it was a compound of Ibsen,

Chekhov and Pinero, with a dash of Barrie and Noel Coward.

"It's tragic in parts and comic in parts and it's—well, it's a little obscure in other parts and it's got a sort of undercurrent of whimsy that's terribly touching. Oswald hopes that it will go on to the West End after this."

"I see," said Mrs. Brown doubtfully. "I'll put a few drops of lemon juice with the sardine, I think. You're the heroine, of course?"

"Of course," said Ethel simply.

Ethel was probably the worst actress who ever trod the boards even of an amateur stage, but she had that particular combination of blue eyes, red-gold hair, oval face and wistful mouth that made the choice of anyone else as heroine impossible.

"And who's the hero?" said Mrs. Brown.

"Well, the hero's is a small part but very important. Oswald explained that there's just a touch of Bernard Shaw in the hero . . . I think that in the end Lionel will have it."

"Oh, Lionel!" said Mrs. Brown without enthusiasm.

Lionel Fenchurch was a youth who had lately come to live in the neighbourhood. He was pleasant and good-looking and capable and immeasurably self-assured. He had attached himself to the band of Ethel's admirers and had already, in the short time during which he had lived in the village, made fairly good headway. Ethel was capricious and imperious and high-handed and kept her admirers generally in a state of bemused uncertainty, but there was no doubt that Lionel, impervious to snubs and set-backs, was gradually gaining ground over his rivals.

"He's rather charming, you know," said Ethel meditatively, as she spread a piece of bread with a mixture of cream cheese and chopped celery.

"Plausible," corrected Mrs. Brown, removing a backbone from the sardine and lemon juice mixture.

"It probably comes to the same," said Ethel, assuming a woman-of-the-world air as she daintily sampled a small piece of cheese and celery on the tip of one finger. "It tastes awfully good . . . Anyway, I like him and he's simply crazy about me."

"I know he is," sighed Mrs. Brown.

"Dorita Merton has been flinging herself at his head for weeks and he just won't look at her. . . . Of course, Archie's dying to be in it, but he's too awful."

Mrs. Brown thought of Archie, the artist who inhabited a cottage—in a state of permanent and unbelievable chaos—at the further end of the village.

"Poor Archie!" she said. "Now he really *is* devoted to you, Ethel."

"I know," said Ethel. "He's been cadging for a part in the play ever since he heard of it, and we did try him for a part but—honestly, Mother, he was just too dreadful."

"I'm sure he did his best, dear."

"Yes, that was what was so dreadful. He did his best and it was just awful. We tried him for the hero's part because the hero hasn't really very much to say. You should have heard him! He had to say, 'I am a criminal, a common criminal, and the net is closing round me. Unless I can flee the country before to-night, I am doomed!'"

"What an odd speech!" said Mrs. Brown.

"Well, it comes into the play," said Ethel. "Oswald

says there's just a touch of Ibsen in it—an atmosphere of lurking menace, you know—and Archie read it as if he was one of those people shouting out the trains at a station over a loud speaker."

"I always think they do it so nicely," said Mrs. Brown.

"Yes, but they aren't supposed to put any Ibsen into it, and Archie was. I believe that he's half demented now he's heard about the party and hasn't been invited and knows that he isn't going to be in the play, but I can't help that."

"Couldn't you just ask him to the party, Ethel?" said Mrs. Brown.

"No," said Ethel firmly. "It's a party for people connected with the play and Archie's not going to be in the play. He did ask if I was expecting him and you should have seen his face when I said I wasn't! Anyway, I think that Lionel must definitely have the hero's part. You see, there's the question of the seat."

"The seat?"

"Yes. That's one of the Barrie touches in the play. There's a seat in the garden by a yew hedge and people who sit on it become the sort of people they would have been if something that had happened hadn't happened or if something that hadn't happened had happened—I forget which. Does that sound very involved?"

"Yes," said Mrs. Brown.

"Well, of course, the Barrie touch always is a little involved. That's the whole point of it. Would chopped onion mix with scrambled egg and mayonnaise? Perhaps not. . . . Well, you see, the seat has got to look a little peculiar. I mean, it's got to suggest magic and mystery and yet be strong enough for people to sit on. It's the sort of thing that Robert would have seen to if he hadn't been away on holiday. Anyway, Lionel said he'd see to it. He's promised to bring it along with him tonight. So you can understand that if he's going to all that trouble over the seat he simply must have the hero's part."

"What does the hero do, dear?"

"He turns into a criminal as soon as he sits on the seat, with a whole crowd of enemies on his track. He's been quite a good man before."

"It certainly does sound a bit odd, dear," said Mrs. Brown placidly.

"Yes, it *is* odd," agreed Ethel. "Oswald says it may be a bit above the heads of the audience, but anyway we've definitely decided that we can't have Archie in it, and I hope he'll stop pestering us. Good Heavens!"—as a tornado seemed to shake the house—"what's that?"

"I think it's only William coming back with the loaf," said Mrs. Brown.

William entered, panting and breathless, a loaf under his arm.

"Sorry if I've been a long time," he said. "I met Ginger."

"Didn't they give you a bag or paper for the loaf, William?" said Mrs. Brown.

"Yes, but it sort of came off."

"It's filthy!" said Ethel as she took the loaf from him. "You might have been playing football with it."

William tried to look as if he had not been playing football with it.

"'Course I haven't," he said. "Well, axshully, it did sort of fall on the ground an' then it sort of got in the way of Ginger's feet an' then it sort of got in the way of my feet an'——"

"And landed in the ditch by the look of it," said Ethel.

"Well, axshully, it did sort of fall into the ditch at the end. I tried to stop it, 'cause I didn't want Ginger to get a goal ... But it's not done it any harm. Why, people *knead* loaves to make 'em, don't they? They bang 'em about, so I bet it's done it good. Anyway, it doesn't matter the outside bein' a bit dirty 'cause you cut off the outside when you make grown-up sandwiches, so you can cut it off now an' I'll eat it to stop it bein' wasted. Well, I'd be helpin' you then, wouldn't I?"

"The only way you can help," said Ethel, "is to clear out."

There was the light of battle in her eye, so William cleared out.

He collected Ginger again and they spent an enjoyable afternoon tracking each other through the wood and trying unsuccessfully to make a weir out of the stream that ran along the edge of it. After that they climbed neighbouring trees and, in the characters of pirate chiefs, carried on a spirited battle from a couple of branches that crossed each other, fell headlong to the ground, carried on the battle there for a few minutes, then, panting and dishevelled, sat back and wondered what to do next. They seemed, for the time being, to have exhausted the possibilities of the wood.

"Let's have another try at sailin' that raft we made over the pond," suggested Ginger.

"No," said William. "I've had about enough water

with that ole fountain. I'm sick of water. It's gone right through me an' out at the other side. . . . Let's go an' practice mountaineerin' up that new house they're buildin'. No one's workin' on it today, 'cause I looked as I came along."

"No," said Ginger. "I've got enough bruises fallin' out of that tree. I've got a double lot with you fallin' on top of me. I've got yours as well as mine an' I'm covered with 'em, same as a Red Indian, an' I'm not goin' mountaineerin' with 'em."

"Let's think of somethin' else then."

They thought for a moment or two in silence, then:

"Let's go to Archie's," they said simultaneously.

The chaos of Archie's cottage held an irresistible fascination for them. Moreover, Archie was a victim of the artistic temperament. He had moods of reckless generosity in which he would shower upon them the contents of his larder and let them riot unchecked among his paints, paint brushes and modelling materials. He had moods of irascibility in which he would drive them furiously from his premises. He had moods of absent-mindedness in which they could take complete possession of his cottage without his even knowing they were there.

"If he's in a good temper we might find somethin' to eat in his larder," said William. "I'm jolly hungry after all that water."

"Yes, an' I'm jolly hungry after all those bruises. Come on!"

Archie appeared to be in a good temper. He saw them coming from his studio window and was standing at the door when they reached it, a radiant smile on his thin, bearded face.

"Oh, good afternoon, boys," he said. "You've brought a note from Ethel?"

"No," said William, "we've not brought a note from Ethel."

Hope struggled with despair in Archie's countenance.

"A message, then?" he said. "You've brought a message from Ethel?"

"No," said William, "we've not brought a message from Ethel."

Gloom closed over Archie. His smile vanished and a look of despondency took its place.

"Oh, dear!" he said.

"Why d'you want a message from Ethel, Archie?" said William.

"I hoped——I hoped she might be asking me to her party tonight," said Archie.

"That ole party!" said William contemptuously. "You needn't worry over that ole party, Archie. It's only for people that are in that rotten ole play."

"I know," sighed Archie, who all day had been hoping against hope to receive a note from Ethel offering him the hero's part and asking him to her party.

"It's goin' to be jolly dull," said William. "They aren't goin' to do anythin' but talk."

"I know," sighed Archie.

"Gosh! The way they talk!" said William. "Fancy a party with nothin' but talk! We've got a jolly good game called 'Lions an' Tamers' an' I offered to fix it up for them an' show 'em how to play it an' they wouldn't even listen. Can we go an' have a look at your larder, Archie? Jus' have a look at it, I mean. An' if there's anythin' you don't partic'ly want . . ."

D

"No!" said Archie, turning upon William the resentment he felt against life in general. "I'm busy. Go away."

"Yes, but listen, Archie——" began William then stopped short, finding that he was addressing the closed door.

"Gosh!" said Ginger. "Well, he's *not* in a good temper."

"It's 'cause he's not been asked to Ethel's party," said William after a moment's consideration. "Grown-ups are always mad when other people don't ask them to their parties. They don't want to enjoy them. They jus' want to be asked. They're bats."

"Well, let's go away till he's got over it," said Ginger. "Let's go'n' practise javelin shootin' with our clothes-prop. My mother's out."

"All right," agreed William. "We'll give him about an hour. I 'spect he'll have got into a good temper by then. I 'spect he's feelin' the pangs of remorse already."

But Archie was not feeling the pangs of remorse. He was engaged in re-adjusting his life. Now that Ethel had finally spurned him, the only course left him was, he decided, to become a world-renowned figure, lonely and wearily disillusioned, on the highest pinnacle of fame. People would know that there was a tragedy in his past. It would be rumoured that he had loved once only and in vain, but there would be something about him that would hold vulgar curiosity at bay. Ethel would hear of him—acclaimed and courted as the greatest artist of the times—and perhaps she would find it in her heart to regret that she had shown him so little appreciation.

The first thing to do, of course, was to start climbing

the pinnacle of fame. He went into his studio and stood looking disconsolately at the pictures that were stacked against the wall. As an artist, Archie hovered uncertainly between the conventional and the "modern". He painted pictures that old ladies said were "sweetly pretty", pictures that represented ivy-covered mansions with peacocks posed on the terrace steps, or dogs of uncertain breed rescuing smiling curly-headed children from precipices; and he painted pictures that represented nothing at all. In neither style had he achieved any measure of success. He turned his frowning gaze from a picture called "Hours of Innocence", in which a white-robed maiden, who bore a vague likeness to Ethel, picked flowers in a garden where daffodils, snowdrops, roses and dahlias rioted exuberantly in defiance of nature, to a picture composed of a triangle with eyes in the corners and a chimney-pot and a pair of gloves hovering uneasily above them. It hadn't got a title yet because Archie hadn't yet decided what it meant.

No . . . reluctantly he had to admit that neither of these would bring him fame. He had submitted them to several exhibitions already, and they had been turned down each time. Then his brow cleared . . . Sculpture . . . If he couldn't be famous as a painter, he would be famous as a sculptor. Ethel should hear of him recognised everywhere as Epstein's rival. That worm Lionel Fenchurch should hear of him, too. He gave a harsh, bitter laugh as he thought of that worm Lionel Fenchurch, who was now, he supposed, prac-tically certain of the hero's part in the play.

He went down to the shed at the bottom of the garden where he did his sculpture and in which stood a roughly-hewn piece of stone. Actually it was Archie's sole attempt at sculpture and he had stopped work on it some weeks ago because he couldn't decide whether to make it classical or modern. If he stopped work on it at the point he had reached, it would be modern and, if he finished it, it would be classical. His eyes brightened as they fell on it. Yes, it was a fine piece of work, he told himself. It had strength, majesty, simplicity and mystery. Mystery, particularly. He was glad that he had told no one about it. It would burst unheralded upon an astonished world. Of course there were a few practical problems to be solved first, among them the precise manner of introducing it to the astonished world. . . . Suddenly he remembered that the Hadley Annual Art Exhibition opened in a few days' time and as yet he had submitted nothing to it. His lips curled scornfully. A provincial art exhibition was indeed a poor field for a sculptor of his standing, but even Epstein, presumably, had had to begin somewhere.

He returned to the cottage and rang up the secretary of the Hadley Art Exhibition.

"It's Archibald Mannister speaking," he said. "May I submit a piece of statuary for the exhibition?"

"Yes, Mr. Mannister," said the secretary on a slightly apprehensive note. "What does it represent?"

"A reclining figure," said Archie.

"I see," said the secretary flatly. "Well, today is the last day for entries, so, if it doesn't arrive by this evening, I'm afraid that we can't include it."

"It shall arrive by this evening," said Archie coldly.

The man did not seem to realise that he was speaking

to one of the greatest sculptors of the age. Then it occurred to Archie that all great artists met with discouragement in their early days. In fact, the man's casual manner was in itself almost a proof of his, Archie's, genius.

"We don't collect exhibits, you know," said the secretary. "You must make arrangements for delivery yourself."

"Of course," said Archie with quiet dignity.

He put the receiver down and turned his attention to the question of delivery. The local carrier, Mr. Crumbs, was notoriously erratic. Sometimes he didn't turn up at all, and, when he did turn up, he was not infrequently the worse for drink. The last time that Archie had engaged him to deliver a painting to the Hadley Art Exhibition, he had delivered it to the local pet shop and left a parrot in a cage on the steps of the Hadley Art Exhibition.

The firm of carriers in Hadley was more expensive but more reliable. He rang them up and, still on the note of quiet dignity, made arrangements for the statue to be collected at eight o'clock. That would give him time to make any small alterations that occurred to him. Then his quiet dignity deserted him . . . and he knew that the pinnacle of fame would be dust and ashes in his mouth without Ethel. He remembered that there was a point towards the end of the play when the hero took the heroine in his arms and pressed his lips upon her brow. He decided to make a last desperate effort. He rang up Ethel.

"Ethel," he said eagerly, "I've thought of a better way of saying those lines. . . . No, do listen. . . . Please . . . I've thought of a different tone of voice

and everything . . . Listen, Ethel . . ." His voice
rose to a high-pitched bleat. "'I am a criminal, a
common criminal and the net is closing round me.
Unless I can flee the country before tonight I am
doomed.' Is that better, Ethel? . . . No? . . . Oh,
dear! I'd hoped . . . I mean . . . Oh, dear!"

Ethel had put her receiver down so he put his down
too, staring at it with an expression of blank despair.
Then he decided to go and have another look at his
Reclining Figure. It would be known to posterity as
Archibald Mannister's first masterpiece. Fantastic
prices would be paid for it after his death. On second
thoughts perhaps he'd keep it and leave it to Ethel in
his will. It would be an heirloom in her family,
descending to her children and her children's children,
together with the story of his hopeless passion, his deep
and unrequited love. . . .

William and Ginger surveyed the broken clothes-
prop gloomily.

"Well, I didn't do anythin' but jus' brandish it an'
hurl it," said William. "It mus' have been a jolly
rotten clothes-prop. Mus' have had somethin' wrong
with it to start with. She ought to be jolly grateful
to us for findin' out about it, before it fell on her head
an' broke her neck or somethin'."

"Well, she won't be," said Ginger. "She'll be mad.
Let's put it somewhere where she won't find it for a
bit an' go away quick."

"All right," said William. "Let's go'n' see if
Archie's got back into a good temper. P'raps he'll give
us a new clothes-prop if he has."

"I bet he won't be in a good temper," said Ginger

GINGER STAYED BY THE GATE WHILE WILLIAM CROUCHED
BENEATH THE OPEN WINDOW AND LISTENED.

gloomily, "an' I bet she'll stop my pocket money
for it."

"Well, we won't waste time on him if he isn't in a
good temper," said William. "We'll jus' go'n' see."

They approached the cottage cautiously. Through
the open window they could see Archie sitting at a
table speaking into his telephone.

"Look! He's telephonin'," said William. "I bet I
can tell by the way he's doin' it whether he's in a good
temper or not. You can gen'rally tell what sort of
tempers people are in by the way they're doin' the
things they're doin'. You stay here an' I'll creep up
an' listen."

Ginger stayed by the gate while William made his

way to the open window, crouching beneath it and listening. When he rejoined Ginger, his face was pale, his eyes open to their fullest extent.

"*Gosh*, Ginger!" he panted. "D'you know what he was sayin'? He was ringin' someone up an' tellin' them that he was a crim'nal an' that if he didn't flee the country by tonight he'd be doomed. . . . Gosh, Ginger! Think of Archie a crim'nal an' havin' to flee the country!"

"He *can't* be!" said Ginger.

"But he said it himself. He said: 'I'm a crim'nal an' the net is closin' round me an' unless I flee the country before tonight I'm doomed.' So it *mus'* be true. An' he sounded in an awful state about it. Sort of *desp'rate*, he sounded."

"Well, is he gettin' ready to flee the country?" said Ginger. "He's not got much time if he's got to do it by tonight."

"I dunno," said William. "I jus' heard him say that, then I came back to you. . . . Come on. Let's go'n' see what he's doin'."

"All right," said Ginger.

They approached the cottage door and knocked. There was no answer.

"P'raps he's fled," suggested Ginger.

"Don't be a chump," said William. "We'd have seen him fleein'."

"He might have fled out of the back."

"Let's go'n' see if we can find any clues. There was a man in a book I once read who could tell that someone had fled through a garden jus' by lookin' at the leaves on the bushes. He was keen-eyed an' hawk-faced."

Trying to look keen-eyed and hawk-faced, the two made their way round the cottage to the little back garden.

"I'll have a look at the leaves on the bushes," said Ginger. "I've not got a microscope, but"—taking a small pocket compass from his pocket—"I'll use this instead."

"Don't be a chump," said William again. "I can see him in that shed an'—Gosh! He's got a great statue there, too."

Ginger reluctantly abandoned his investigations.

"I'd nearly got a clue that he'd gone out of that gate," he said.

"Well, he hasn't because he's there. He hasn't seen us yet . . . We'd better not tell him we know he's a crim'nal."

"Why not?"

"People gen'rally murder people that find out they're crim'nals. They jus' put 'em out of the way, case they tell the p'lice."

"Gosh!" said Ginger apprehensively. "P'raps we'd better not go near him."

"No, we've got to try'n' help him get out of this net that's closin' round him. He's our friend an' we've got to help him."

Archie's long thin form appeared suddenly in the doorway of the shed.

"What are you two boys hanging about for?" he said. "I thought I'd told you to go home."

"We—er—we jus' came back to see how you're gettin' on, Archie," said William, entering the shed. "You see——" He caught sight of the statue and stopped short. "Gosh, Archie! What's that!"

"GOSH!" SAID WILLIAM. "IT DOESN'T LOOK LIKE A
RECLINING FIGURE TO ME."

"Can't you see what it is?" said Archie irritably. "It's a statue."

"Yes, I know," said William, all thought of Archie's criminal career driven out of his head by the amazing object before him, "but what's it of?"

"It's a reclining figure."

"*Gosh!*" said William. "It doesn't look like a reclining figure to me. It doesn't look like anythin'. What's that part sticking up at the end?"

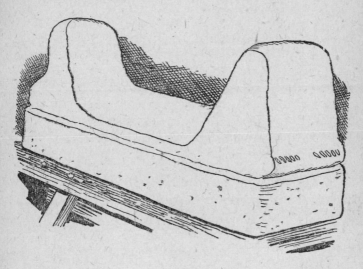

"It's reclining on its elbow. That's its chest and head."

"It hasn't got a face," objected Ginger.

"It isn't meant to have a face," said Archie testily. "It doesn't *represent* a reclining figure. It *expresses* it. Don't you know anything about modern art?"

"No," said William.

"It's not meant to represent the object at all. It's meant to suggest the emotions aroused by the thought of the object."

"Oh . . ." said William. "Well, what's that stickin' up at the other end?"

"That's the knees," said Archie. "The knees are raised. The figure is reclining on its elbow with raised knees."

"Oh . . ." said William. "Why's it got one great leg 'stead of two ordin'ry ones?"

Archie looked at the massive rough-hewn limb with a mixture of irritation and uncertainty. He had been tempted at one point to chisel a line down the middle in order to suggest a pair of legs, and then had dismissed the impulse as pandering unworthily to the naturalistic school. But he still wasn't quite sure.

"I've just explained," he said in exasperation. "It doesn't represent legs. It represents the idea of legs."

"What are those funny wriggly marks at the end of it?"

"They represent the idea of toes," snapped Archie. "And now what have you come for? I'm very busy today."

"We know you're busy, Archie," said William. "We've come to help."

"Help?"

"Yes," said William, exchanging a significant glance with Ginger. "We thought we could sort of help you with your packing."

"Packing?" said Archie with an annoyance in which William thought he detected guilt and discomfiture.

"Yes. . . . You—you're goin' away, aren't you, Archie?"

"Certainly not," said Archie.

"You mean—you mean you're goin' to stay here, 'spite of everythin'?" said William. "I mean, after what's happened?"

"Of course I am," snapped Archie.

That his repulse by Ethel (which filled his whole mental horizon) should be considered so final and should be so widely known that he was expected to leave the neighbourhood on account of it was a humiliating and outrageous thought.

"If you think," he continued, "—if anyone thinks —that I'm going to be driven away by a little thing like that——"

"It seems a jolly big thing to me," said Ginger.

"Perhaps it does," said Archie, "but you know nothing of the circumstances and, anyway, it isn't your business."

"I know it isn't," said William. "We're only tryin' to help, an'—— Listen, Archie. Ginger an' me'll pack for you in two minutes. You won't want many things. Jus' your pyjamas an' a toothbrush. Come to that, you can do without pyjamas an' toothbrushes."

"Will you boys clear out?" said Archie savagely. "If you don't clear out, I'll—I'll—I'll——"

"All right, Archie," said William. "We'll clear out."

The two went down to the road.

"Gosh, he was jus' goin' to murder us," said Ginger. "Well, we've done everything we could an' he won't go."

"Poor ole Archie!" said William. "I 'spect he jus' doesn't know how to flee a country. He'll jus' stay here till this net closes right round him. Well, we've got to help him."

"How can we?"

"We've got to get him out of the country somehow. He's been jolly good to us. D'you remember the time he let us play with his lay figure an' wasn't angry when its head came off?"

"Yes."

"Well, then, we've *got* to get him out of the country before this net closes round him."

"Yes, but how *can* we?" said Ginger again. "We can't drag him down to the station an' *push* him into a train."

"N-no, I s'pose we can't. Anyway—— Gosh! I never thought of that till jus' this minute."

"What?"

"They're prob'ly watchin' the stations. That's what he meant by the net closin' round him. That's why he won't go. He's goin' to stay in his cottage at bay. He'll prob'ly take poison or shoot himself when he sees Scotland Yard comin' in at the gate. Well, we've jus' *got* to do somethin'."

"You keep sayin' that," said Ginger, "but I don't see there's anythin' we *can* do."

William looked up and down the road. Almost opposite Archie's cottage stood the Blue Lion and outside the Blue Lion stood Mr. Crumbs' van. That was no unusual sight. The space outside the Blue Lion was the usual parking place of Mr. Crumbs' van.

"*Look!*" said William.

"Look where?"

"Mr. Crumbs' van . . . Scotland Yard'll be watchin' the stations, but it'll never think of Mr. Crumbs' van."

"Yes, an' I bet Mr. Crumbs wouldn't help him flee the country even if you told him about it."

"I'm not goin' to tell him about it. I've got a bit

more sense than that, with Archie's life hangin' by a thread. Why, he'd start tellin' everyone about it and it'd get round to Scotland Yard in no time. I'm jus' goin' to find out where he's goin', that's all."

At this moment the portly figure of Mr. Crumbs appeared in the open doorway of the Blue Lion. He held a mug of beer in his hand and wore his usual air of jocund good humour.

William assumed his most wooden expression as he approached him.

"WILL YOUR VAN BE HERE TILL SEVEN, MR. CRUMBS?"
ASKED WILLIAM.

"Good afternoon, Mr. Crumbs," he said.

Mr. Crumbs' large rubicund face creased into a smile. "Good arternoon, young 'un, an' how are you?"

"Very well, thank you, Mr. Crumbs. . . . You—you've got a jolly good van there, haven't you?"

"She ain't too bad," said Mr. Crumbs, surveying his ramshackle vehicle with an indulgent eye.

"I s'pose you go some—well, some pretty long journeys in it, don't you?"

"Sure I do," said Mr. Crumbs.

William's expression became blanker and more wooden than ever.

"When's the nex' long journey you're goin', Mr. Crumbs?"

"Well, I goes to Portsmouth tonight," said Mr. Crumbs.

"Ports——? Gosh! That's where the sea is, isn't it?" said William excitedly.

"Yes, it's by the sea," said Mr. Crumbs. He chuckled. "But I ain't got no time fer paddlin' nor buildin' sand castles. Goin' down empty an' fetchin' a load back to Hadley."

"What time will you be starting, Mr. Crumbs?"

"Seven or thereabouts," said Mr. Crumbs. "Got a fancy fer night drivin'. Them there zebras ain't all cluttered up with blinkin' pedestrians an' you can get a move on."

"An' will your van be here—jus' where it is now—till seven, Mr. Crumbs?"

"Likely it will," said Mr. Crumbs blandly as he turned to re-enter the Blue Lion.

William rejoined Ginger, his eyes alight with excitement and determination.

"Gosh, Ginger! He's goin' to Portsmouth, so if we can get Archie on the van he can flee the country all right. He can get straight into a ship as a stowaway an' he'll have escaped this net that's closin' round him."

"Yes, an' how're we goin' to get Archie on the van?" said Ginger.

"Well, it doesn't start till seven an' I bet he'll have thought things over by then an' re'lised that he'd better get out of this net before it closes. It'll be nearly dark by then, too, so there'll be more chance of him gettin' away without Scotland Yard knowin' about it, 'case they're hidin' somewhere an' watchin' out for him."

"Well, we can try," said Ginger doubtfully, "but I dunno that it'll come off."

"'Course it'll come off," said William. "We'll meet here at seven an' get him in. I *bet* it'll come off."

But even William felt a little apprehensive as he and Ginger approached the van under cover of dusk and peered into its dim recesses. It was empty except for a potted hydrangea and a large bottle.

"There's heaps of room for Archie," whispered William. "He can spread out an' go to sleep an' have a nice rest before he begins stowin' himself away. Come on. Let's start tryin' to get him on it."

"*That's* goin' to be a job," said Ginger.

"Well, let's start it, anyway."

They went up to the cottage door and knocked. Archie opened the door and stood looking down at them severely.

"You again?" he said. "What do you want now?" William cleared his throat.

"There's—there's a van come for you, Archie," he said hoarsely.

"Oh, yes," said Archie, peering into the dusk. "It's rather early, but I'm quite ready."

William gaped at him. . . . The ease with which the difficulty had been surmounted took away his breath. Archie, so recalcitrant only an hour ago, was now evidently prepared to flee the country without protest.

"Oh . . ." said William. "Well—er—are you comin' to it now?"

"I must get the statue."

"Gosh, Archie!" gasped William. "You're not takin' that great big statue with you, are you?"

"Of course I am," said Archie and vanished abruptly into the back regions of the cottage.

William turned to Ginger.

"He mus' be bats!" he said. "Fancy anyone what's fleein' the country takin' a great big statue like that with them. He won't be able to flee an *inch* with that great big statue."

"I dunno," said Ginger thoughtfully. "It might be a sort of disguise. I mean, if he's got that statue with him, Scotland Yard'll think he's a sculptor an' not a crim'nal at all."

"Y-yes," agreed William, "but it's goin' to be a jolly heavy disguise to lug about with him all over the place. He may have to flee right round the world an' I bet he'll get jolly sick of luggin' that ole statue with him."

"He can always chuck it into the sea or somewhere if he gets tired of it," said Ginger. "Come on . . . Let's see what he's doin'."

They tracked Archie to the garden shed, where he stood, hatted and coated, gazing in a harassed fashion at his Reclining Figure.

"Are you ready, Archie?" said William.

"Yes . . ." said Archie.

"I don't know about that statue, Archie," said William doubtfully. "I don't think you'd better take it with you."

"Of course I'm going to take it with me," said Archie. "There'd be no point in going without it."

"No, I suppose not," said William. "I mean, I s'pose you're goin' to sort of pretend you're a sculptor."

"I *am* a sculptor," said Archie with chilly dignity, then the familiar note of anxiety returned to his voice. "The only trouble is how to get it on to the van. Actually, I wasn't expecting the van for an hour or so yet and——"

"Look, Archie!" said Ginger. "There's the men that have been mendin' the road comin' along. P'raps they'll lend a hand."

Encouraged by Archie's largess, the road menders lent rough but ready hands. They hoisted up the Reclining Figure and slung it into the van, smashing the bottle and utterly demolishing the potted hydrangea. Archie clambered up after it and sat, panting and harassed-looking, by his masterpiece. It never occurred to him to doubt that this was the van he had engaged to convey him and his Reclining Figure to the Hadley Art Exhibition. Archie had a one-track mind. He had ordered a van and a van was here. He inquired no further.

William and Ginger stood at the door of the van and watched him anxiously.

"I'd leave that statue behind if it gets in your way, Archie," advised William.

"Of course it won't get in my way," snapped Archie. "I don't know what you're talking about. There's ample room."

"Yes, but I mean when you're fleein' . . ."

"There's lots of ships in Portsmouth, you know, Archie," said Ginger reassuringly.

"Yes, I know that there are lots of ships in Portsmouth," said Archie irritably. "What an idiotic thing to say!"

"I expect you've — made plans, haven't you, Archie?"

"Of course I've made plans," said Archie more gently as roseate dreams of his future career floated once more before his eyes.

"I dunno that it's goin' to be easy findin' room for that great big statue, all the same," said William.

"Of course I'll find room for it," said Archie. "I tell you, I've made all the arrangements."

"You mean, you've got people to help you?" said William.

"Of course I've got people to help me."

William looked at Archie with a new respect, visualising him meeting masked and cloaked confederates, creeping into the coal bunkers of a shadowy vessel. . . .

"I say, Archie," he said suddenly, "can we come with you?"

"Of course not," said Archie. "I shan't have any time for bothering with children."

"No, I know you won't, Archie," said William humbly, "but——"

Archie was looking round the van, puzzled by its continued immobility.

"Where's the driver?" he said. "He has the directions, of course, but——"

At that moment Mr. Crumbs emerged from the door of the Blue Lion, gave a quick glance into the interior of the van, then climbed into the driver's seat.

"Good!" whispered William to Ginger. "He didn't notice Archie an' the statue."

The engine started up and the van moved slowly down the road.

William and Ginger stood looking after it sadly.

"It may be the las' time we'll ever see Archie all the rest of our lives," said William with a deep sigh.

Mr. Crumbs had noticed Archie and the Reclining Figure, but he was in a slightly fuddled state and could not quite disentangle the events of the evening.

Mr. Lionel Fenchurch had approached him in the bar of the Blue Lion with inquiries as to his route. He passed the Browns' house on the way to the Portsmouth road, didn't he? Well, if he, Mr. Lionel Fenchurch, put a flowering plant and a bottle of champagne in the van, would Mr. Crumbs kindly stop at the Browns' house and deliver them? Mr. Crumbs, after reflection and the receipt of a handsome tip, said that he would. It appeared that Mr. Lionel Fenchurch had intended to go to a party at the Browns' house, that unforeseen circumstances had prevented his going, and that he wished to soften the blow of his absence by a little offering. Mr. Lionel Fenchurch had, it

"GOOD HEAVENS! IT'S ARCHIE!" EXCLAIMED ETHEL,
PEERING INTO THE VAN.

seemed, a strong sense of the dramatic. He didn't
want his offering to be delivered tamely before the
party began. He wanted it to be delivered when the
party was in full swing, announced by Mr. Crumbs:
"A present for the party from Mr. Fenchurch." But
Mr. Crumbs' brow was puckered in bewilderment as he
drove down the road. Looking into the van, he had
seen neither plant nor bottle. All he had seen was a
young man and a statue. Perhaps he had misunder-

stood Mr. Fenchurch. Perhaps Mr. Fenchurch had
said a young man and a statue when Mr. Crumbs had
thought that he had said a flowering plant and a bottle.
Perhaps Mr. Fenchurch had added the young man and
the statue as an afterthought, taking for granted that
the tip would cover both, as indeed it well might.
Anyway, Mr. Crumbs decided that he would stop at
the Browns' house, deliver his load and see what
happened. With luck, it might mean another tip. . . .

He drew up at the Browns' gate and looked at the
lighted windows. It was clear that a party was in
progress, but there seemed to him to be little evidence
of the party spirit. No music or laughter. Only a
buzz of earnest conversation.

Mr. Crumbs was right.   There was little evidence of the party spirit at the Browns' party.   Lionel had rung up at the last minute to say that he was sorry not to be able to come but that he was in bed with a cold . . . and Oswald Franks had seen him (with his own eyes, as he repeatedly affirmed) entering Hadley's foremost hostelry with Dorita Merton, both dressed to kill and obviously intending to spend the evening at the "dinner and dance" that was in progress there.

"Dorita Merton!" said Ethel, her voice quivering with anger.   "The plainest girl I've ever seen in my life!   Her eyes don't match, even."

"Well, he certainly can't have the part after this," said Oswald grimly.   "And there's the seat. . . ."

"What about the seat?"

"He said he'd see to it and have it all ready for today, and he's done nothing about it.   *Nothing!*   I taxed him with it this morning and he admitted it. It was quite clear that he hadn't even given a thought to the matter."

"We won't have him in the play at all," said Jameson, who took the part of an ancient butler who knew an important secret but had lost his memory.

"Certainly we won't," said Ronald Bell, who took the part of a wealthy uncle returning home in heavy disguise to put his relatives to the test.

"Here's old Crumbs' van drawing up at your gate," said someone, "and old Crumbs is getting out of it and coming up to the door."

"I'd better go and see what he wants," said Ethel.

She opened the front door.   The rest of the party crowded behind her.

"Is it something for us, Mr. Crumbs?" said Ethel.

"Yes, miss," said Mr. Crumbs.   He had only a vague memory of the message entrusted to him but strove gallantly to deliver what he remembered of it.   "Something fer your party . . .   Leastways, I think so."

"What can it be?" said Ethel.

"What *can* it be?" clamoured the guests.

They swarmed down to the gate and clustered round the van, peering into its dim recesses.

"It's Archie!"

"Good Heavens!   It's *Archie!*"

"And what on earth has he got with him?"

"Look!   It's the seat!"

"He's got the seat!"

"Oh, *Archie!*"

"And all the time Lionel was talking about it and doing nothing Archie has been quietly working on it."

"And finished it in time to bring along to the party."

"Isn't it lovely!   It's just right.   It's got just that touch of magic and mystery."

"Archie, you're wonderful!"

They drew out Archie, blinking and beaming.   He didn't know what had happened, but here he was in the centre of the party, with Ethel saying he was wonderful. . . .

Willing hands heaved out the Reclining Figure, and set it in the Browns' hall.   Everyone in turn sat on the shapeless stomach, resting arms or elbows on the rough-hewn head or knees.

"How did you think of it, Archie?   It's just right."

"And you didn't say a *word*.   You just quietly set to work on it."

His thin face wearing a perplexed but radiant smile, Archie was wafted into the sitting-room, offered drinks and cheese straws. . . . Archie was vague but not quite devoid of sense. As he basked in Ethel's smiles and gratitude, he wisely decided to say nothing about the Hadley Art Exhibition.

Mr. Crumbs had gone on his way, driving a van that was now empty except for a wrecked hydrangea plant and a broken champagne bottle. Archie had found time to slip a ten-shilling note into his hand before he left and he felt well satisfied with his evening's work. Still—it was all a bit mysterious. Could those nippers have had anything to do with it? They'd been hanging about the van, he remembered. Then he dismissed the problem from his mind and abandoned himself to the pleasure of a night drive over zebras uncluttered by blinking pedestrians.

The van had long vanished from sight when William and Ginger approached the Browns' house. They walked slowly and spoke in hushed conspiratorial tones.

"I bet he'll have got to Portsmouth by now."

"I bet he won't. It's a long way off, is Portsmouth."

"I wish he hadn't taken that great big statue with him. I bet he'll find it jolly diff'cult stowin' himself away on a ship with a great big statue. I've never heard of a stowaway takin' a statue with him, have you?"

"No. Still, if they're watchin' the ports for him it'll put them off the scent all right."

"Yes, he'd ev'dently got it all thought out. I say, Ginger . . ."

"Yes?"

"People'll wonder what's happened to him. They'll think it jolly funny, him jus' vanishin' an' leavin' no trace. D'you think we ought to tell someone?"

"I dunno. . . . P'raps we'd better keep it dark till he's finished fleein' the country. He may send us a postcard. In a disguised hand, of course."

"P'r'aps we ought to tell Ethel. I bet he'd want Ethel to know."

"Well, we can't tonight, anyway, 'cause of the party."

They stood at the gate and looked at the lighted windows. Sounds of laughter and animated conversation floated out into the evening air.

Ginger heaved a mournful sigh.

"Jus' think what they'd feel like," he said, "if they knew that Archie was on his way to Portsmouth, fleein' the country with the net closin' round him."

"Gosh, yes," said William, gazing at the festive scene through the uncurtained windows. Suddenly his mouth fell open. "*Gosh!* . . . There's someone there that looks like . . . It *can't* be . . ."

"Can't be what?"

"Archie. . . . It *can't* be . . ."

"'Course it can't be. Archie's on his way to Portsmouth, fleein' the country with a statue."

"I'm goin' in," said William shortly.

He entered the house and stood at the open door of the sitting-room. The statue now held place of honour in the middle of the room, with Oswald Franks sitting on it in a negligent attitude. Archie stood on the hearth-rug, a look of seraphic happiness on his face. Ethel sat near him, smiling up at him sweetly.

"I've thought of another way of saying those lines, Ethel," he was saying. "Listen. How would it be if I said them like this?" He sank his voice to a hollow moan. "'I am a criminal, a common criminal, and the net is closing round me. Unless I can flee the country by tonight, I am doomed.'"

They all laughed and applauded.

"He must have the part now, mustn't he, Ethel?"

"Of course he must."

William rejoined Ginger in the hall. There was mingled consternation and disappointment in his expression.

"I say, Ginger, it was somethin' out of a play he was sayin' on the telephone. It wasn't real at all."

"Gosh!" said Ginger. "D'you mean he's not fleein' the country?"

"'Course he's not."

"And we've taken all that trouble for nothin'."

"Yes."

Suddenly Archie's eyes lit on the two boys and a thoughtful look came over his face. Like Mr. Crumbs, he was wondering exactly what part those two nippers had played in the mysterious events of the evening. He made his way over to them.

"Hello, boys," he said a little nervously. It occurred to him that it might be best not to inquire too closely into what had happened. . . . Still, they had certainly had a hand in bringing about the present situation and for that, at any rate, he owed them gratitude. "Is there —er—is there anything I can do for you?"

"You couldn't give me a new clothes-prop, could you, Archie?" said Ginger tentatively.

"A clothes-prop?" said Archie, startled. "Well, no, I'm afraid I couldn't, but here you are."

He plunged his hand into his pocket, put two coins into Ginger's hand and rejoined the laughing group by the fire.

William and Ginger retired to the staircase and sat on the bottom step, morosely contemplating the two coppers that Archie (by now completely and justifiably flustered) had given them in mistake for two half-crowns.

"It doesn't rep'sent a tip," said William bitterly. "It jus' rep'sents the emotions roused by the thought of a tip."

"Yes," said Ginger. "We've worked jolly hard an' nothin's turned out real. . . . Archie's crime wasn't real."

"The statue wasn't real."

"An' now the tip isn't real."

William was silent as a distant memory grew clearer and clearer... Crisp, crunchy pastry with a delectable circle of raspberry jam in the middle.

"Well, I know somethin' that *is* real," he said. "Come on to the larder."

CHAPTER V

WILLIAM AND LITTLE YUBEAR

"WHAT shall we do this afternoon?" said Ginger. William and Ginger were in William's bedroom, watching a downpour of rain that blotted out the countryside.

"The pond'll be full an' it'd be a good day for me to practise bein' a diver," said William, "but I'd better not do it for a bit. My mother was mad on Thursday."

On Thursday William, bent on perfecting himself in his chosen career as a diver, had donned a homemade diving suit, consisting chiefly of trays and saucepans from his mother's kitchen, with the addition of a few empty tins from the dustbin and a length of garden hose from the tool-shed, and dropped from the tree that overhung the pond into its murky depths. He had been rescued by a passer-by and taken home, sodden with pond water and encrusted with slime, having left a good part of Mrs. Brown's kitchen equipment behind him.

"No," he continued regretfully, "I'll have to wait till she's forgotten about Thursday before I start practisin' bein' a diver again."

"What shall we do, then?" said Ginger.

"Tell you what!" said William. "Let's go on with the story."

In the intervals of their more active pursuits,

William and Ginger were writing a story. Or rather, William was writing the story, while Ginger took the part of appreciative audience, making occasional suggestions that William generally ignored.

"Yes, let's," said Ginger. "It's a long time since we did it. I've forgot what it's about now."

"You're always forgettin' what it's about," said William testily. "It's the most excitin' story I've ever wrote an' you keep forgettin' what it's about."

"Well, I get muddled," said Ginger, "an', anyway, it keeps changin'. It started with pirates an' then it went on to Guy Fawkes an' then it turned pre-historic an' then it got to gangsters an' smugglers an' then it went to the atom bomb an' I've forgot where it is now."

"You've got an awful mem'ry," said William. "It's got to the best part of all now. It's about that king of a foreign country that got turned out by villains that had got a man that was the double of the real king an' were tryin' to make him king 'stead of the real one. This double was a jolly deep villain, too, but they couldn't crown him king 'cause the real king had gone off with the crown jewels an' so this double couldn't be crowned king without the crown an' so he's come over after the real king to try 'n' get the crown off him so's he could be crowned an' that's where we'd got to the las' time we wrote it."

"Yes, I remember now . . ." said Ginger.

"Well, let's go on with it," said William. "I thought out a lot more in hist'ry class yesterday while ole Frenchie was talkin' about some industrious revolution or other. It didn't seem to have any excitin' battles in it, so I stopped listenin'."

He went to a drawer, took out a grubby exercise

book and a short pencil, chewed, in his moments of mental stress, to an almost unrecognisable shape and consistency, examined the "point" critically, bit away some more of the wood to expose the lead, then lay down on the hearth-rug on his stomach (his usual position for creative work) and began to turn over the pages.

"We'd got to where this king had got the crown jewels hid in an empty house an' this double was after them."

"Yes, but hadn't he got swallowed by a crocodile?" said Ginger.

"No, you chump, that was the Red Indian Chief— the one that had lost all his money bettin' on horses at Monte Carlo an' was fleeing the country with Scotland Yard after him."

"Oh, yes, I remember, but——"

"You see, this double wanted the crown jewels so's he could be crowned king."

"Oh, yes. . . . But, listen, I thought he'd fallen down a precipice out of an aeroplane."

"No, you chump, that was the smuggler what had kidnapped the customs man so's he wouldn't be able to stop him smugglin' things into the country an' it jolly well served him right, fallin' down that precipice!"

"Yes, but——"

"Oh, shut up talkin' so much. I want to get on with the story. I've got to have quiet for my brain to work. All great story writers have to have quiet for their brains to work. I bet that's why I've never finished a great story, 'cause my brain never gets any quiet."

"Well, it's you that's always makin' the noise," Ginger reminded him mildly.

This statement was so true that William forbore to contradict it.

"Int'ruptin' your own brain," said Ginger, developing the theme.

"Well, shut up now, anyway," said William. "I can feel my brain startin' to work . . . An' stop breathin' on me. People breathin' on your brain stops it workin'."

Ginger withdrew to a respectful distance and watched his friend with mingled pride and interest as William, his brow corrugated with thought, his tongue protruding with mental effort, began to write in the grubby exercise book, scoring the paper so deeply in his earnestness that the ragged point of the pencil tore large holes in the pages as it worked its way across them.

"There!" he said at last, sitting back to survey his efforts. "I've had 'em meetin' at the gate of the empty house where the king's hid the jewels an' the double's goin' in to look for them. Gosh!" with deep satisfaction. "I've made them say some awful things to each other. . . . You can read it now if you like."

Ginger craned his head over William's shoulder and read:

They staired at each other in garstly raige you cink of inickwitty said the dubble pail with gilt you blaggard steaped in krime said the king in a nobel voice but bewear your dume is ceiled and your days are gnumbered I will rase an army and waid in your blud the villan shuke with fere at the nobel words but nuntheless he went on his villanus way into the house to fulphil his dedly purpus.

E

"It's jolly good, isn't it?" said William complacently.

"Yes, it is," said Ginger, impressed, "but why doesn't the king stop this double goin' into the house?"

"Well, he's not got time. He's goin' to raise an army same as he said. Anyway, I want the double to go into the house. . . . Tell you what! I've got another idea." He chewed the pencil, absentmindedly spitting out the pieces that became detached in the process. "I'll have a ghost in the house. The ghost of one of the people the double's murdered an' it'll come out an' scare the double while he's lookin' for the jewels. . . . I'll start writin' it now quick while I've got my brain goin'."

He took up his position again at full length on the hearth-rug, knit his brows, extended his tongue . . . and once more the stubby pencil gnawed its way across the pages, while Ginger withdrew to a respectful distance to watch him.

"There!" said William at last, relaxing the tension of brows and posture. "You can read it now. I think it's jolly good."

Again Ginger leant over his friend's shoulder and read:

Just as the dubble started his dasterdly serch the silance of the house was broke by a hollo mone a gost sed the dubble harf mad with terrer speek huever you are the speckter gave anuther garstly grone the dubbles blood kurdelled and his hare stood on end speek he sed again his voice horse with frite.

"It's jolly good, isn't it?" said William again, complacently.

"Yes, it is," agreed Ginger. "Did it speak?"

"No, it didn't," said William, "but it scared him so he gave up lookin' for the jewels. He's an awful coward, is this double, you see."

"I bet he wouldn't give up lookin' for the jewels even if he *is* a coward," said Ginger. "I bet he wouldn't give up jus' for a ghost. He'd know they're only made of air, are ghosts. They can't do anythin' to you."

"They can kill you with fright," said William. "People find you dead in the haunted room nex' mornin' with a look on your face what they carry the mem'ry of to their dyin' days. I've read stories about it."

"Well, stories aren't the same as real life," persisted Ginger. "I bet he'd stay an' look for the jewels in real life."

"I bet he wouldn't."

"I bet he would," said Ginger.

"All right. Let's try. Gosh, yes! That's a good idea," said William, his spirits rising. Despite his literary leanings, he was not a boy who found inactivity of any sort congenial, and he was already tiring of creative effort. The idea of combining the working out of his plot with the occupations of ordinary life appealed to him strongly. "We'll find a villain— same as this double—an' get him in an empty house searching for some crown jewels an' I'll pretend to be a ghost an' scare him, an' we'll see what he does."

"Y-yes," said Ginger, bewildered, as usual, by the speed with which William laid his plans and the deceptive simplicity the problem assumed in the process. "But I bet it's not goin' to turn out as easy as that."

"Yes, it is," said William, rising to his feet and putting exercise book and pencil back into the drawer. "It's stopped rainin' so all we've got to do is to find a villain an' get him in an empty house searchin' for crown jewels."

"Who'll we find for the villain?" said Ginger, forgetting his misgivings as interest in the adventure gripped him.

"Oh, there's lots of villains about," said William carelessly. "We'll think of the villainest one we can. . . . I know! Hubert Lane!"

"Gosh, yes! Hubert Lane!" said Ginger excitedly. "An' we owe him one, too, for that choc'late he gave us with pepper in."

"Huh!" said William. "I *like* pepper in choc'lates. I knew there was pepper in it an' I ate it 'cause I like pepper in choc'lates, so that was snooks for ole Hubert Lane. Anyway, we'll have him for the villain, all right."

"Then we'll have to find an empty house," said Ginger.

"There's that empty house called Elm Mead at the end of the lane," said William. "The one we played in las' Sat'day. We can get in by that back window same as we did then. We didn't have time to go right over it, but it's a jolly good empty house. It's the sort of empty house I'd like to live in. It's got that flat bannister-top for slidin' down an' that ladder goin' up to the loft an' a staircase you can make more noise goin' up an' down on than any empty house I've ever come across. I don't see any *sense* coverin' stairs up with carpets. You can't make any noise on carpets. An' puttin' furniture all over the place!

When I'm grown up I'm goin' to live in an empty house with no curtains an' no carpets an' no furniture an'——"

"Well, about this villain," said Ginger, seeing that William was mounted on one of his favourite hobby horses, and trying to unseat him before it was too late. "We ought to get it fixed up quick."

"Yes, 'course we ought," said William, dragging his mind from roseate visions of a lifetime spent in an empty house. "Anyway, wc've fixed up Hubert Lane for the villain. We'll tell him about tryin' to be king of a foreign country an' havin' to get these crown jewels out of the empty house, then I'll go in first an' hide somewhere an' make a noise like a ghost an' watch how he carries on."

"I bet he'll jus' run away."

"We won't let him. I'll get in through the window an' unbolt the door an' hide somewhere an' you stay outside an' shut the door soon as he's got in an' keep it shut so's he won't be able to get out. He's too fat to get out through the window, anyway. Gosh! It'll make a jolly good story. I bet it's goin' to be one of the best stories I've ever wrote."

"Yes, I b'lieve it is," said Ginger, infected as usual by William's enthusiasm. "Let's go 'n' have a look at the house now."

The setting sun twinkled at the windows of the empty house in a way that seemed to encourage their enterprise.

"It's got a sort of haunted look to start with," said William. "I bet I can act a ghost better than any real ghost. I say! It would be a jolly good idea to start hauntin' a ghost. I bet it wouldn't know how to haunt back at someone what was hauntin' *it* an'——"

"Yes, but how'll we fix Hubert Lane up to be the villain?" said Ginger, hastening to interrupt William before he got carried away by this new theme.

"Oh, yes . . . ole Hubert Lane. . . ." said William. He looked round the darkening landscape. "It's too late to start now. It's bedtime an' my fam'ly makes an awful fuss when I don't come in 'zactly at bedtime. Gosh! the fuss grown-ups make about goin' to bed! When I'm grown up I'm not goin' to bed at all. I'm goin' to stay up all night. I've thought out some jolly good games for playin' at night. I bet——"

"When'll we tell Hubert Lane about it?" said Ginger.

William glanced down the road. A short fat figure was coming towards them through the dusk.

"There he is!" said William. "I'll tell him now."

As Hubert recognised them, a sickly smile spread over his puffy face and he stood hesitating, poised for flight. But the tone of William's "Hello, Hubert" reassured him. Evidently the little matter of the peppered chocolate had been forgotten or forgiven. Encouraged, he began to think up further little tricks . . . mustard in an ice cream . . . pebbles in a dough-nut . . .

"Hello, William," he said. His oily smile went from William to Ginger. "Hello, Ginger! How are you?"

"I say, Hubert," said William, "we've jus' heard somethin' excitin' about you. You're jolly lucky."

"Me?" said Hubert eagerly.

William cleared his throat then plunged into the recital.

"YOU'VE GOT TO LOOK FOR THE JEWELS IN THIS HOUSE,"
SAID WILLIAM.

"Yes, you're the double of someone that's king of a country an' jus' been turned out an' if you can get hold of the crown jewels you can get crowned king of this country an'—an'——"

Hubert was staring at him, open-mouthed with amazement but by no means incredulous. Hubert's credulity was his weak point. He was mean and cunning and sly but he believed everything he was told as long as it appealed to his sense of self-importance. The oily smile vanished from his face and his eyes goggled.

"Me?" he said again.

"Yes," said William. "We can't tell you how we got to know 'cause it's all a tangle of international pol'tics an' crime, but all you've got to do is to go an' hunt for them in this empty house where they're hid, an' find 'em."

A look of uncertainty had come over Hubert's face. There were some stories, of course, too tall even for Hubert to swallow. Then, just in time, William remembered another of Hubert's weaknesses.

"Gosh, Hubert! Think of bein' a king! You can

eat as many cream buns as you like. You can jus'
never stop eatin' cream buns all the rest of your life."
Hubert gulped greedily and William hastened to pursue
his advantage. "An' if you don't like anyone you can
jus' clap 'em into dungeons or drive 'em into exile."

Hubert's eyes gleamed. Vindictiveness was another
of Hubert's pleasant little failings.

"I'll do more'n that," he said. "I'll chop 'em into
pieces."

"Yes," agreed William. "Well, jus' think, Hubert.
You'll have a jolly good time if you can find those
crown jewels an' get crowned king—eatin' cream buns
an' choppin' people into pieces all day long."

"Well, where *are* they—these crown jewels?" said
Hubert. "Tell me where they are."

"You've got to look for them in this house," said
William, pointing to the empty house, which was
hardly visible through the falling dusk, "but it's too
late now. It's so dark you wouldn't be able to find
anythin'. So you'd better start first thing tomorrow
mornin'. An' you mustn't tell anyone, 'cause, if you
did, your enemies'd be on your track an' they'd get
those jewels before you'd time to look for 'em."

"No, I won't tell anyone," said Hubert, his face
glowing with happy anticipation. "I'll have ice cream
an' cream doughnuts an' choc'late creams an' jam tarts
an' I'll hang my enemies on trees in the garden before
I start cuttin' 'em up."

"Yes, Hubert," said William, "you're goin' to have
a jolly good time . . . Well, g'bye."

"G'bye," said Hubert, vanishing into the dusk.

"Gosh, isn't he awful!" said Ginger.

"Yes, but I bet he'll turn up all right," said William

with satisfaction. "I did that jolly well, didn't I? I've got a jolly lot of tact. I've a good mind to be one of those men in the government called dip— something."

"Dipsomaniacs?" suggested Ginger vaguely.

"I 'spect so . . . Anyway, I'm goin' to be one when I grow up. It's not so messy as divin' an' it'd leave me more time for goin' to the moon an' explorin' countries never yet trod by the foot of man an' things like that.

"Yes, but what about tomorrow an' ole Hubert?" said Ginger.

"Oh, yes," said William, bringing his mind from the ever-increasing complications of his future career to the matter in hand. "Well, I'll come to this empty house first thing in the mornin' an' find a good place to haunt him from an'—an' if it's not goin' to be jolly excitin' I'll be surprised."

"So'll I be," said Ginger with a faint note of appre-hension in his voice.

Early the next morning William approached the unoccupied house. It seemed still to wear a cheerful friendly air as if anxious to co-operate with him in his adventures. The kitchen window slipped open easily. He entered the small empty room without mishap and made his way into the hall and up the stairs. And then, when he was half-way up the stair-case, he got his first shock. There came the unmistak-able sounds of a large vehicle drawing up in the road outside, and the sound of voices. Startled, William looked out of the window.

A removal van stood at the gate and from it were

PANIC-STRICKEN, WILLIAM RAN UPSTAIRS TO THE TOP
LANDING

descending a woman, a little girl and a couple of
removal men. The woman and the little girl made
their way up to the front door. The men began to
lift a chest of drawers and a collection of depressed-
looking potted plants from the van. There followed
the sound of a key turning in the lock and the voices
of the woman and the little girl in the hall.

The unoccupied house was unoccupied no longer.

Panic-stricken, William looked round for escape.
Impossible to descend the stairs—the woman and the
little girl were there in the hall just beyond the bend
of the staircase. Impossible to climb out of the
window—the removal men were in possession of both
road and garden. Obeying the blind impulse of flight,

William continued his way to the top landing. But already there was the sound of footsteps on the stairs below him as the men started to heave up the chest of drawers.

"Just put it anywhere," called the woman. She sounded vague and placid and absent-minded. "It doesn't really matter where anything goes. We can sort things out later."

"Oh, look, Mummy," said the little girl. "There's a dear little cupboard under the stairs. Can I play shop in it?"

"Yes, dear," said the woman.

Heavy footsteps continued to ascend the stairs. Again William looked desperately round for escape. Just above his head was a trap-door leading into a loft and, leaning against the wall, beneath it, was

a ladder. In a few seconds William had put the ladder in position, prised open the trap-door and pulled himself through the opening.

He found himself in a small loft that held a water cistern and an accumulation of rusted household goods, evidently put there by the previous tenant as the simplest way of disposing of them. Crouching among the dust and cobwebs, William held the trap-door slightly open and watched the scene below. The men moved to and fro with the furniture. The woman flitted aimlessly about, murmuring, "Put it anywhere. It doesn't really matter."

The little girl had found a basket of provisions and had taken it into the cupboard to stock her "shop", where she was keeping up a brisk trade.

"Ten and six a pound for rice, Mrs. Jones," she said, "and we'll send it round to your house. . . . The tea's a penny a packet, but you can have it for a half-penny if it's your birthday."

After a time the removal men sat down on a chest on the landing, took out packets of sandwiches and began to munch them. The woman hovered about, talking in a rambling, desultory fashion.

"I've been in such a muddle getting ready for the move that I don't know whether I'm on my head or my heels," she said. "I'd arranged for a French boy to come and stay a fortnight and I believe he was supposed to arrive today but, when I realised that it was the day of the move, I wrote to the boy's parents to change the day to next week. I only hope they got the letter in time. I'm not even sure I remembered to post it because everything's been in such a muddle. . . .

"I don't know the French boy, of course, but he's anxious to improve his English and I thought it would be a good opportunity for my little girl to learn French, though I don't suppose that either of them will really learn anything. Children don't, you know . . . And actually it's even more complicated than that. I wrote to three agencies because I wanted to make sure of having a French boy, and all three wrote to say they'd send one, so I wrote to two of them to tell them not to. At least, I meant to write, but I'm not sure whether I actually *did*. I've even forgotten the boys' names. Still, it's no good worrying over these things, is it?"

"No, 'm," said one of the men.

"It's care what killed the cat," said the other.

"Biscuits are a penny a bite," shrilled the little girl from the cupboard. "Big bites twopence. . . . Yes, madam . . . Certainly, madam. . . . We deliver in your road every hour with a horse and cart. You can have a ride on the horse for sixpence."

"If they come they come, and if they don't they don't," said the woman. "That's the only way of looking at it, isn't it?"

"Yes, 'm," said one of the men.

"Bridges is best not crossed till you come to 'em," said the other.

Then Hubert entered by the front door.

Hubert was a boy whose brain worked slowly. He had been told that this was an empty house. He had seen for himself last night that it was an empty house. Therefore it remained in his eyes an empty house and he dismissed the signs of occupancy as immaterial. He entered with a lordly air as if already feasting his eyes on heaped mountains of cream buns and rows of his enemies dangling from trees.

"Oh, dear! Here's one of them," said the woman. "I suppose his luggage is coming later." She approached Hubert with a vague smile of welcome. "There you are, dear! What's your name?"

"Hubert," said Hubert.

"You've got quite a good English accent," said the woman, "but I want you to feel at home, so we'll call you Yubear. That's how your name is pronounced in *la belle France*, isn't it? I'm Mrs. Hart and—Susie!" The little girl came out of the cupboard and stared resentfully at Hubert. "This is Susie, my little girl. We're in a bit of an upset, as you see, but you won't mind that, will you, Yubear? Just occupy yourself as best you can till the furniture's in, then we'll see to you. . . . Go with him, Susie dear, and look after him."

Hubert glanced around, then entered the front room, overlooking the garden. Susie trailed after him slowly.

"Learn all the French you can from him, dear," called her mother as an afterthought.

William lowered the trap-door and stood for a moment, considering the situation. It had got so far beyond him that there didn't seem to be anything he could do about it. He turned a rusty pail upside down and, standing on it, opened the skylight and looked cautiously out.

Ginger's figure could be seen lurking in the bushes at the bottom of the garden. Ginger, too, was finding the situation beyond him. He had come to close the door of an empty house on Hubert Lane in order to prevent his escape from William's hauntings and discovered, instead, a house full to overflowing, as it seemed to him, of removal men, women and children. He had taken refuge in the bushes and was waiting the course of events. William's figure, appearing suddenly out of the skylight and gesticulating frantically, roused him from his stupor.

"What'll I do?" he called in a hoarse whisper.

The wildly waving arms seemed to be beckoning him indoors . . . then the pail collapsed and William vanished.

William picked himself up and opened the trap-door again. The situation was more or less unchanged. The removal men were still carrying pieces of furniture into the house. The woman was still telling them to put them anywhere, and the little girl was following Hubert from room to room with increasing resentment. At intervals she went to her mother to report his movements.

"He's looking in all the drawers and cupboards, Mummy."

"Yes, dear," said Mrs. Hart. "The French are a nation full of intellectual curiosity. It's a well-known fact."

"Mummy, he's found your jewel-case and he's trying your pearl necklace on his head."

For Hubert, having failed to find his crown, was experimenting with various possible substitutes.

"Probably a French custom, dear," said Mrs. Hart, unconcerned.

"He's trying the soap dish on his head now, Mummy."

"Probably another French custom, dear."

"I don't like him, Mummy."

"We must try to cultivate the spirit of international brotherhood, dear," said Mrs. Hart absently as she carried a small table into the dining-room from the hall then back again into the hall.   "I don't remember where this went in the old house.   As a matter of fact I don't remember it at all, but it must have been somewhere. . . .   We are all members of one large family, dear. . . .   Oh, there's that old biscuit box.   I lost it years ago. . . .   We must stretch hands of friendship across the sea."

"Can't you send him home, Mummy?"

"Who, dear?   Little Yubear?   No, of course not. He's our guest.   In any case, it's a most complicated rail service."

The little girl went up to the front bedroom, where Hubert was ferreting about in a suit-case that contained Mrs. Hart's toilet requisites.   The little girl's pent-up exasperation broke its bounds.

"You leave our things alone," she said fiercely. "You go back to where you came from.   I don't want you here."

Hubert raised his head and looked at her.   She was very small and very slight—an ideal antagonist from Hubert's point of view.

"D'you know what I do to people I don't like?" he said with oily pleasantness.   "I hang 'em up on trees an' then cut 'em up into little pieces."

"Leave my mummy's things alone."

She tried to snatch the case from him.   He seized her wrist and gave it an expert twist.   She hit out at him, then ran from the room in sudden terror.   The ladder seemed the nearest way of escape.   She scrambled up it. . . .   Miraculously the trap-door

WILLIAM EMPTIED **THE PAIL FULL ON HUBERT'S PUFFY**
UPTURNED FACE.

opened and William's hand pulled her up the last and most difficult part of the ascent. He closed the trap-door.

"There's a horrible boy down there," she said. "He twisted my wrist."

"All right," said William.

He lifted the door a trifle and peeped down. Hubert was beginning to manœuvre his plump figure up the ladder in pursuit of his victim. William filled the rusty pail from the cistern and emptied it full on the puffy upturned face. Hubert fell howling to the ground and fled downstairs, colliding with Ginger, who was just coming in at the front door. Ginger had decided to venture boldly into the house and at all costs join forces with William. The impact of Hubert's drenched figure disconcerted him.

"Get out of my way!" he said.

"You get out of mine!" bellowed Hubert.

Fear and anger had lent Hubert an unusual degree of courage and the two wrestled furiously in the door-way for a moment before Hubert fled down the garden and over the countryside, closely pursued by Ginger.

Mrs. Hart, who was unpacking a crate of china in the dining-room, looked up to see the two flying figures pass the window.

"The other two French boys perhaps," she said. "Or perhaps not . . . Anyway, one can't do anything about it," and returned to unpacking the china.

Upstairs in the loft the little girl was gazing round with interest.

"I haven't been up here before," she said. "It's a nice place, isn't it? Is that the water cistern?"

"Yes," said William. He splashed about, sending

streams of water on to the floor. "They're jolly int'restin' things, are water cisterns. I once got right into ours at home, tryin' to find out how it worked, but they made an awful fuss. . . . Have a drink out of it in your hands. It tastes jolly good. It's better than when it comes out of a tap."

They drank noisily of the dust-infested surface, sending fresh streams of water on to the floor.

"Yes, it is jolly good," said the little girl. "I like its funny taste."

Again William looked round the small cobwebby loft.

"Ginger an' me once played bein' pirates in a submarine up in our loft," he said. "We didn't get right into the tank, but we pretended it was the sea."

"Let's play that," said the little girl.

"All right," said William. "I'll be the captain an' you can be the crew." He assumed a commanding position, legs apart, arms folded, and spoke in a gruff bass voice.

"Avast there! Heave to an' weigh the anchor an' splice the mizzen!"

"Aye, aye, sir," said the little girl.

"Ship ahoy! Avast again an' back the main top an' hoist the periscope an' fire a volley of torpedoes to leeward of yon sloop laden with stolen treasure!"

"Aye, aye, sir," said the little girl.

"Fire aboard. All hands to the pump!"

"Aye, aye, sir," said the little girl, taking up the rusty pail from the floor.

The game continued. Though small and slight and of the sex for which William professed scorn and abhorrence, she was an admirable playfellow.

Downstairs the removal men, touched by Mrs.

Hart's helplessness, had taken complete charge of operations, making what they considered a tasteful arrangement of furniture in each room.

Mrs. Hart wandered upstairs and looked at the pool of water beneath the trap-door of the loft and the trickle of drops that was descending into it.

"The cistern's leaking," she said. "It's an odd thing but I've only got to move into a house for the cistern to start leaking. I've noticed it over and over again."

She spoke without rancour. She was merely stating a fact.

The work of arranging furniture and unpacking china made steady—if slow—progress. The submarine game exhausted itself. The little girl remembered a tin of sugar-coated biscuits somewhere among the household equipment that flowed and ebbed like a tide over the floor of hall and kitchen, and went down to look for it.

She found her mother gazing up at the trap-door with an expression of mild surprise.

"It seems to have stopped leaking," she said. "I wonder what's happened. . . ."

"The boy's been doing things to it," said the little girl.

"The boy?"

"The boy in the loft," said the little girl.

"Oh, yes, little Yubear. . . . I'd forgotten. How clever of him!"

"'Scuse me, 'm," said one of the removal men. "This bit o' furniture seems to've got broke."

"I expect it was broken before," Mrs. Hart reassured him. "It's the revolving bookcase, isn't it? It always revolved too quickly for me to get the book I wanted. I never liked it."

"WEE," SAID WILLIAM, BARING HIS TEETH IN A GLASSY
SMILE.

"Well, some likes 'em an' some don't," said the man.

"Takes all sorts to make a world," said his colleague.

The little girl failed to find the sugar-coated biscuits but she returned to the loft with a hunk of bread and cheese—the remains of the men's lunch—which she and William divided and ate with much enjoyment. But they were tiring of the loft and their thoughts were turning to the rest of the house—still unexplored and full of possibilities.

"There's a sort of sliding door between the sitting-room and the dining-room," said the little girl as she swallowed the last morsel of bread and cheese. "It runs along a little tunnel in the ground an' goes right back into the wall. I saw it when we came to look over the house, but I hadn't time to try doing anythin' with it."

"Let's try now," said William. "Let's try clangin' the palace gates in the face of a rebel army. You be the rebel army an' I'll be the king. Then you can be the king an' I'll be the rebel army."

"All right," said the little girl happily.

It was the resounding crash of the sliding doors that brought Mrs. Hart into the room. Susie and a strange boy were dragging the doors again across the floor. She was puzzled for a moment; then recollection returned. The French boy . . . little Yubear. He had seemed fatter and of a different colouring on their first meeting, but she knew that her memory was unreliable. She took herself in hand. It was time she had a little talk with him.

"Well, Yubear, dear," she said. "Do you like England?" She stopped and continued slowly and laboriously, "*Aimez-vous Angleterre?*"

William turned round. His rule in a crisis was to take the line of least resistance. Someone was addressing him in French, so he replied with the only French word that he had securely at his command.

"*Wee*," he said, baring his teeth in a glassy smile.

Mrs. Hart continued to address him in anglicised and laborious French. She asked him if he had had a pleasant journey, if he felt quite well, if he enjoyed living at his home in Aix-les-Bains—he *did* live at Aix-les-Bains, didn't he?—and if he thought he would be happy at Elm Mead. At each question William bared his teeth in the glassy smile and replied *"Wee,"* becoming so carried away by his rôle that he began to press his elbows against his side and spread out his fingers in what he fondly imagined to be a foreign gesture.

Vaguely satisfied, Mrs. Hart murmured *"Au revoir pour le présent"*, and drifted into the garden, where the men were wrestling with a wire mattress that had become entangled with a fireguard and a clothes line.

It was at this moment that Mrs. Brown stopped at the gate. She was returning from a shopping expedition in which she had managed to secure all her favourite brands of groceries, and some darning wool that exactly matched the rather difficult shade of Robert's new socks. Her husband had just won the Golf Club Tournament Cup and William had been behaving in such an exemplary fashion since his unfortunate immersion in the village pond that the eternal hope of a permanent improvement was already springing in her breast. . . . And so she felt at peace with all the world and ready to give a helping hand to anyone who needed it.

"Do let me . . ." she said, entering the garden and setting to work on the clothes line.

The mattress and fireguard seemed suddenly to give up the struggle, and the men carried them indoors.

"Moving *is* an ordeal, isn't it?" said Mrs. Brown.

"It is," agreed Mrs. Hart. "It was complicated enough to start with, and now that Yubear's arrived it's still more complicated!"

"Yubear?" said Mrs. Brown mystified.

"Yes. A little French boy from Aix-les-Bains. I've just been having a chat with him in French. My

French must be better than I thought because he understood everything I said."

"Is he staying here?" said Mrs. Brown.

"Yes, he's come as a paying guest for a fortnight to improve his English. I'd fixed today for him to come and then when I found out that we were moving today I put him off. At least, I meant to; but the letter can't have reached him because he's arrived. At one point two other boys seemed to have arrived as well—I'd written to three agencies—but I think they were chiefly local and it boils down to little Yubear. He's a most intelligent child. The cistern was leaking and he mended it."

Mrs. Brown smiled.

"That's wonderful. It's more than my small boy could have done."

"But Heaven only knows where he's going to sleep tonight," said Mrs. Hart. "You see what a muddle we're in!"

"I'll put him up with pleasure," offered Mrs. Brown. "I have a small boy, too, you know, so he can share his room. Does he understand English?"

"He seems to . . . That's terribly kind of you. It would be a great relief to me. Won't you come indoors and meet him?"

Mrs. Brown threaded her way through the various impedimenta that littered garden path and hall till she reached the dining-room. All that could be seen of the small boy and girl who occupied it was their back views as they knelt on the floor examining the mechanism of the sliding door, which seemed to have been put out of action by the latest assault of the rebel army.

Mrs. Hart crossed the room and laid her hand on the boy's shoulder.

"Our French guest," she said. "Little Yubear from Aix-les-Bains."

William turned round, and the glassy smile he had prepared for the visitor froze on his face.

Mrs. Brown looked down at the familiar freckled features and gave a gasp.

"*William!*" she said.

William's mind worked quickly. Before him was his mother, her amazement already giving place to wrath. Behind him was an open window.

Ginger, coming in at the front gate, narrowly escaped being hurled to the ground by the fleeing figure.

"I've given Hubert a jolly good bashing," he said, "an'——"

"Come on, quick!" panted William, hardly pausing in his flight.

"What's happened to him?" said Mrs. Hart, gazing round the room. "Where's Yubear?"

"It was William," moaned Mrs. Brown.

"Yes, but where *is* he?"

William had reached the comparative safety of his bedroom. Retribution was on his track, but, before it overtook him, he must set down the result of his experiment. Through all the tangled skein of the day's adventures, he had kept in mind the thread of his story and he wanted to tie up the end of it before it became too inextricably entangled.

Still panting, his grubby face set and scowling with effort, his tie awry, his dishevelled hair entwined with cobwebs, his person soaked in cistern water, he lay on the hearth-rug writing with concentrated energy. Ginger sat by him watching him expectantly.

"There!" said William at last, handing him the exercise book. "You can read it now."

Ginger took the book and read:

The dubble fled roring with raige and ringing his hands in frite but not before he had savidgely attackd a pore maden leeving her for ded but a nobel frensh hero kame to her resku and together they saled a pirat submareen and klosed the pallice gaites on a rebble army she wasent a bad maden as they goe.

to be kontinyoud

CHAPTER VI

WILLIAM THE NEW ELIZABETHAN

"WE ought to be doin' somethin' about bein' New Elizabethans," said Henry.

"Who are they?" said William.

"Well, they're the same as old Elizabethans but they're new," said Henry.

William digested this piece of information in silence, then said "Oh."

"Well, you see," said Henry, trying to elucidate the theme, "they had a Queen Elizabeth then an' they did things for her in a sort of historical way an' we've got a Queen Elizabeth now so we've got to do things for her in a sort of modern way."

"Oh," said William again, but this time there was interest and even earnestness in his voice.

Since watching the Coronation on television, William had been consumed by a secret fervour of loyalty. As liege man of life and limb, he would have yielded place to no one.

"Well, let's start, then," he said in a purposeful business-like voice.

"What'll we do?" said Ginger.

"I bet all the things they did were jolly dangerous," said Douglas.

The four were walking down the road towards the field that led to the old barn, armed against possible foes by a bow and arrow, a catapult, a water pistol and a pea shooter.

"We could form an army," said Ginger reflectively. "We'd make a better army than grown-ups, 'cause we're smaller an' could move about quicker under bushes an' things. We could shoot at 'em from a long way off an' get away before they could shoot back."

"Yes," agreed William, "that's jolly sens'ble. An' there's small soldiers called gerkins that are the best soldiers in the world."

"Gurkhas," said Henry. "But these Elizabethans I'm thinkin' of didn't so much fight as adventure."

"We'll adventure, then," said William. "We've had a jolly lot of practice in adventurin'."

"What sort of adventures did they do?" said Douglas doubtfully.

They had reached the old barn now, and they sat down on the ground looking expectantly at Henry.

"One of them was called Drake," said Henry.

"I know about him," said William. "He fought a battle called the Armada."

"An' he played a game," said Ginger.

"Bowls," said Henry, "an' when the Spaniards came he said, 'There's time to finish the game an' beat the Spaniards, too'."

"It's a rotten game, bowls," said William. "I've got an uncle that plays it. They jus' roll 'em along the ground 'stead of throwin' them prop'ly. Now darts . . ."

His voice was tinged with bitterness. Robert had recently taken up darts with all the enthusiasm of youth, and had last week acquired a dart board. Aware that the great desire of William's heart was to test his prowess on it, he kept it locked up when not in use and refused to allow William even to hold the darts, caddy fashion, when he was practising.

"Darts!" repeated William. "It's a wizard game. I bet I could beat 'em all at it if they'd let me try As if I could do 'em any harm, jus' throwin' 'em! I expect Robert's afraid I'd beat him. I bet——"

"Well, about this Armada," interrupted Henry, knowing that William, once embarked on this particular subject, could hold forth on it indefinitely if unchecked. "We can't do that adventure 'cause it was a sea battle an' there isn't any sea here."

"Couldn't we make it a land battle," suggested Ginger, "an' couldn't we make Hubert Lane an' his gang the Spaniards? Gosh! We owe the Laneites somethin' for that trick they played on us las' Saturday."

Last Saturday Hubert Lane and his gang, overhearing William and Ginger planning to practise vaulting over the gate of Five Acre Meadow in order to perfect themselves in their careers as acrobats, had smeared the rungs of the gate with creosote and watched the result from the shelter of the hedge with malicious delight.

"Yes, let's have 'em for Spaniards," agreed William. "We jolly well *do* owe them something."

"No, that won't do," explained Henry patiently. "They aren't foreigners. The old Elizabethans only fought foreigners, so we've got to do the same as they did. Anyway, Hubert Lane's gone away to stay with his godmother an' I don't know when he's comin' back."

"We'll get even with 'em all right when he does,"

said William grimly. "Well, what did this Drake do besides fightin' that battle called the Armada?"

Henry considered.

"He took treasures off foreigners an' brought them home for the country," he said.

The sombreness of William's visage lightened.

"We could do that, all right," he said.

They looked at him in faint—only faint—surprise. They were accustomed by now to William's inexhaustible optimism, but it never failed to give them this first slight feeling of bewilderment.

"How?" said Ginger.

"We'll jus' find foreigners an' take treasures off them," said William airily. He turned to Henry. "How did this Drake do it?"

"He did no cruel deed," said Henry, quoting his history book. (Henry was the only one of the Outlaws who gave any serious consideration to the study of history.) "He jus' went about takin' 'em. . . . Once he found someone asleep with bars of silver by his side so he jus' took 'em. Another time he found some llamas—that's foreign for donkeys—with silver on 'em so he jus' took it. An' he brought it home to give to the country."

"That's what we'll do, then," said William in the tone of one who has solved a problem to the entire satisfaction of everyone concerned. "We'll take treasures off foreigners an' bring 'em back for the country."

"How'll we give 'em to the country when we've got 'em?" said Ginger. "It's a long way to Parliament an' we don't even know its address."

Frowning, William considered this objection, then the frown cleared from his face.

"I bet the Mayor of Hadley 'd do," he said. "He can take 'em up to London with him nex' time he goes. He's called Mr. Kirkham an' I know where he lives. He's jolly nice. He once bought me an ice cream."

"Yes, but how'll we get the treasures off foreigners?" said Douglas. "We've got to find foreigners with treasures on 'em to start with, an' I bet it won't be easy to get 'em off 'em when we do. I don't b'lieve there *are* any foreigners round here, anyway."

"Yes, there are," said William. "Mrs. Monks has got a foreign maid."

"Well, that's only one an' I bet she's not got any treasures."

"I heard my mother say that a retired Anglo-Indian Colonel had taken Reeth Lodge over at Marleigh," said Ginger. "He mus' be a foreigner."

"Anglo means English," said Henry.

"Yes, but Indian means Indian," said Ginger triumphantly, "so he mus' be part foreign. We can count him foreign anyway."

"That's two," said William. "It's a jolly good beginning, is two. An' there's no reason why we shouldn't find someone asleep by treasures or donkeys with treasures on 'em same as this Drake did."

"When'll we start?" said Henry.

"Now," said William simply. "We'll all set off diff'rent ways an' get treasure off foreigners an' bring it back here. I'll take this Indian man. I bet he's the most dangerous. If he's a colonel, he mus' be jolly fierce. They're jolly fierce, are colonels. Who'll take Mrs. Monk's maid?"

"I will," said Ginger. "I've seen her. She looks pretty fierce, too."

"We've got to do no cruel deed to 'em, you know," said William.

"I bet they're more likely to do cruel deeds to us," said Douglas with a bitter laugh.

"All right," said William. "If you don't want to be a New Elizabethan, don't be one."

"Oh, yes, I do," said Douglas.

"Who'll you go to, then?"

"There's someone called Mrs. Ducrasne who's come to live on the new building estate," said Douglas. "I bet she's foreign with a name like that."

"All right," said William a little doubtfully. "Well, that leaves Henry. . . ."

"I'll jus' go 'n' try an' find one," said Henry.

"Yes," agreed William. "Drake found 'em so there's no reason why you shouldn't. Anyway, that's what we'll do. We'll go off now an' we'll meet here again in about an hour with the treasures."

"We'd better have a password, hadn't we?" said Ginger.

The Outlaws agreed. They always liked to have a password. It seemed to confer a certain dignity and romance on their exploits.

"We'll have 'God Save the Queen'," said William, "an' we'll come back here in about an hour an' we won't let anyone in without the password."

William walked slowly up the drive of Reeth Lodge. It was an imposing mansion, and the adventure that had seemed so simple and straightforward a few minutes ago began now to seem a little less simple and straightforward. Something of his air of carefree nonchalance dropped from him as he approached the house. His spirits rose, however, as he noticed french windows standing open on to a paved terrace. Entrance, at any rate, was easy, whatever difficulties the later stages of the undertaking might present.

Stepping cautiously on tip-toe, he approached the terrace and entered the french window.

The room in which he stood was large and sombre. There were chairs of unusual wood carved in unusual fashion; ivory and ebony ornaments; Eastern rugs and hangings; native weapons on the wall. A mounted tiger's head, flanked by two polo sticks, glared down at him from over the chimney-piece, but it was not this that made William stop short on the threshold with a gasp of excitement. For there, outstretched on a sofa, fast asleep, was an elderly military-looking old man and beside him on a table stood a large and elaborately fashioned silver elephant, bearing aloft in its trunk a silver vase over the edge of which half a dozen roses drooped dispiritedly. The sleeping foreigner with the treasure by his side. . . . All he had to do was to take it. The thing was so simple that William could hardly believe it was real.

He approached the table, casting cautious glances at the sleeping warrior as he did so. The warrior was certainly an impressive sight. He had a long yellow face, adorned by a flowing white moustache. The moustache, indeed, seemed to flow endlessly, stretching out fierce tentacles five or six inches beyond the sunken cheeks. After inspecting the warrior with interest, William turned his attention to the treasure. It was obviously valuable—beautifully-fashioned, with every detail delicately incised. The country, thought William complacently, would be jolly grateful to him.

F

He was just putting his hands carefully on the base
when the warrior stirred, snorted and opened red-
rimmed eyes.

"Hello, hello, hello," he said, sitting up. "What
are you doing with that?"

"I'm taking it away," said William.

The warrior relaxed again on his couch.

"Take it by all means," he said, waving a hand in
dismissal. "I loathe the thing. It was given to my
wife as a parting present when we left India and I've
loathed it ever since I saw it. Look at the brute's

"I'M TAKING IT FOR THE COUNTRY," SAID WILLIAM.
"I'M A NEW ELIZABETHAN."

face. Look at the smugness of it. Look at the sneer
on it. Take it away, by all means, my boy."

"You don't mind me takin' it?" said William, a
little surprised.

"Not at all, my boy. Not at all. Take it by all
means. Ever since we brought the thing home, I've
hoped against hope that it would be stolen, but the
local burglars have had a bit more sense. Hideous,
isn't it? Hideous. And there the brute stands day after
day with that idiotic look on its face, sneering at me."

"That's all right, then," said William, again placing his hands on the base of the ornament.

"I know nothing about it," murmured the colonel drowsily. "I went to sleep and when I woke up the thing was gone. How should I know where it went or who took it? I dreamed that a boy came into the room but it was only a dream. You're just a dream, my boy, and Jumbo shall sneer at me no more." The red-rimmed eyes followed William's movements as he hoisted up the heavy ornament. "What are you going to do with it, by the way? I don't want to poke my nose into what's no concern of mine but——"

"I'm taking it for the country," said William.

"Excellent, excellent," murmured the warrior, then a startled look came into his face and the ends of his moustache jerked up. "For the country? What d'you mean, for the country?"

"I'm a New Elizabethan," said William. "I'm taking treasures off foreigners same as the old ones did, an' with you being' a foreigner——"

"No, no, no," said the warrior. He brought his feet to the ground and sat with his elbows on his knees, his red-rimmed eyes fixed on William. "No, no, no, you've got me wrong there, my boy. I'm English. English to the backbone. My ancestral home—gone now—was in the West country and the 'mad Hetherleys'—my name, Hetherley, you know—have been famous there for generations, for centuries. The 'mad' rather a compliment than otherwise, you understand."

William's mouth had dropped open.

"You—you're not a foreigner, then?" he said.

"No, no, no. We Hetherleys go back to before the

conquest. Look on William the Conqueror as an up-start. Hunted bears in woad, I've no doubt. Fought on the beach against Julius Caesar. I've no definite authority for that, of course, but—oh, English, all right. English to the marrow."

"But someone said you were an Anglo-Indian," said William a little indignantly.

"Just a figure of speech, my boy. Means I served in India. Any colour suggestive of the Orient you may notice in my face is due to liver. Pure liver. No foreign blood has ever mingled with the Hetherley strain. . . . Now take that wretched thing and go away."

But William had replaced the ornament on the table.

"I can't take it if you're not a foreigner," he said. "We only take them off foreigners."

"I see," said the colonel vaguely. "Oh, well, it can't be helped, I suppose. One of those things that happen. We must both just make the best of it." He glanced out of the window. "Here's my wife coming back. I warn you that she won't take the same view of this incident as I take. She treasures the brute. Polishes it up every day. It's the apple of her eye. . . . In any case, she's not fond of boys. She doesn't encourage them."

William, too, glanced out of the window. The lady who was approaching it had a grim, tight mouth and steely eyes beneath an old-fashioned toque. Her cloak had a martial swing and she grasped an umbrella as though it were a weapon of offence.

"Who's that boy?" she said sharply as she stepped on to the terrace and approached the window.

William slipped out of the window and dodged past her. She made a lunge at him with her umbrella. He fled across the lawn, flung himself through the hedge, fell into the ditch, climbed out of it, mud-stained and bedraggled, and made his way across country to the old barn.

"So, you see, that's what happened," said William. "Everything was all right for it. He was asleep with the treasure by his side—an' it was silver, too, same as the Old Elizabethans—but he turned out not to be a foreigner, so I couldn't take it. It was jolly hard lines. An' this wife of his set on me an' I only jus' got away with my life."

Ginger and Douglas—Henry had not yet arrived—listened with interest to the recital.

"Yes, that was jolly excitin'," said Ginger. "Mine was excitin', too." He raised his hand to his eye, surrounded by a faint blue ring. "But it wasn't as excitin' as yours."

"What was yours?" said William.

"No, let's have Douglas's first."

There was a smug sleek look about Douglas. His eye was not blackened nor his legs mud-stained.

"Well, mine turned out all right in a way," he said, "but I didn't get any treasure. I mean, she turned out not to be a foreigner, too. I told her about it an' she said she wasn't a foreigner an' she was jolly nice about it an' gave me a jolly good tea."

They looked at him suspiciously. Douglas had a way of emerging unscathed from any adventure.

"I bet you knew she wasn't foreign all the time," said William.

"Well, she might have been with that name," said Douglas.

"I'll tell mine now," broke in Ginger. "Mine was foreign all right. Gosh! She *was* foreign! She was cleanin' the stairs an' as soon as she saw me come in at the door an' start lookin' round she shouted at me like mad an' threw the brush at me an' it caught me right on the eye, so I came away then. I could see there wasn't any treasure anyway." Again he fingered his bruise. "I bet it'll be black by tomorrow," he added with modest pride.

"God Save the Queen!" said Henry from the doorway.

"Enter, friend," said William.

"I've not got any treasure," said Henry, entering.

"Neither have any of us," said William gloomily. "I bet there isn't as much treasure about as there was in old Elizabethan days. . . . Well, what did you do?"

"I went along the road," said Henry, "an' I saw two foreigners sittin' by the roadside an' eatin' big rolls with cheese or somethin' inside 'em an' talkin' to each other. I could tell they were foreigners 'cause they were talkin' foreign. Well, they hadn't got any treasure with them so I went on a bit further an' I saw two bicycles propped against a gate with strings of onions on 'em. It seemed jus' like that Drake man findin' donkeys with treasure on 'em so I thought I'd take one 'cause I thought a string of onions would be better than nothin' . . . but, soon as I got hold of it, the two foreigners came up. I tried to 'splain but they couldn't understand an' they talked a lot but I couldn't understand, but they laughed an' were jolly nice an' gave me an apple."

He took an apple from his pocket.

"Gosh!" said William morosely. "All that huntin' for treasure an' only an apple at the end of it!"

"Well, let's eat it," said Ginger. "Let's have bites in turn."

They passed the apple round, munching thoughtfully.

"We'd better give the whole thing up," said Douglas.

"No, we won't," said William firmly. "We've set out to be New Elizabethans an' we're jolly well goin' to be." He turned to Henry. "What else did they do, besides findin' treasure?"

Henry swallowed the apple core and considered.

"They discovered new countries," he said. "Drake discovered one called Virginia."

"We'll discover a new country, then," said William.

"We can't," said Henry. "You've got to go over the sea to discover new countries an' we can't get to the sea. We tried once, you remember. We walked for miles an' miles an' miles an' never came to it."

"You needn't go over the sea to discover new countries," said William. "There's other countries on the other side of the earth, an' I bet they've not found 'em all yet. They've found Australia, but I bet there's lots of others they've not found. Stands to reason if you try to discover new countries by goin' along the top of the earth there's forests an' rivers an' things that you can't get through. I bet there's hundreds of countries they haven't discovered yet."

"Well, how'll we get to them?" said Ginger.

"We'll dig," said William. "It may take us a bit of time 'cause the earth's jolly thick, but we're sure to get through it in the end."

As usual the Outlaws' first faint bewilderment was melting in the light of William's optimism.

"All right," said Ginger. "We'll need spades an' things."

"Yes," said William, "an' we've got to think of a name to call it. Virginia's a silly name. Why did they call it that?"

"It was after the Queen," said Henry.

"We'll call ours Elizabetha," said William. He considered for a moment, then added, "We'll have to take provisions an' a Union Jack to plant when we get there."

"Where'll we start diggin'?" said Ginger.

"Somewhere where people won't see us," said William. "We don't want a lot of people knowin' about it. 'Sides, they'd be sure to stop us if they knew. They always stop us doin' anythin' int'restin'."

"What about Grantham Lodge?" said Henry.

They looked at him in some surprise. Grantham Lodge had been wrecked by a bomb in the last year of the war and was still a mass of ruins and rubble in a large overgrown garden. The property had been bought by the educational authorities, who were planning to build a training college for teachers on the land, but the economy cuts had put an end to their plans, and year by year the derelict property stood there, growing more and more derelict as time went on.

The Outlaws had never used it as a playground. Its connection with the educational authorities and its future as a training college for teachers had invested it in their eyes with an atmosphere of horror that the actual bombing had failed to produce.

"Gosh!" said William. "*That* place!"

"Yes," said Henry. "There's that shrubbery close up to where the house used to be an' it's jolly thick an' there's room in it to dig an' no one'd see us from the road. We could make a sort of camp there, with provisions an' things same as real explorers do."

"Yes," agreed William after a moment's thought. "It's a jolly good idea."

Their arrangements were speedily completed. The wheelbarrow from Henry's garden was packed with spades, shovels, a Union Jack and such provisions as the Outlaws could most easily abstract from their home larders. These comprised half a meat pie, some cold rice pudding, quarter of a jelly, half a jar of anchovy paste, two sardines, a few chicken bones and some sandwich crusts lavishly sprinkled with Gentleman's Relish that Ginger had salvaged from his aunt's bird table. William had provided the liquid refreshment. To quarter of a bottle of orange squash he had added a sauceboatful of gravy, some mint sauce, a spoonful of yoghourt, the remains of a bottle of glycerine (for which he had a special weakness) and a dash of soda water. Shaken up, the result had a curious colour and consistency, but, as William said, "Stands to reason that a lot of tastes taste better than jus' one taste 'cause there's more of them."

The spot that Henry had suggested for their excavation was, as he had pointed out, close to what had once been the side of the house and hidden from the road by thick bushes. Rain had fallen during the night and the soil—a thick loamy soil—yielded easily to their efforts. Their "spades" were of varying degrees of usefulness. William's was a garden spade, taken boldly from the tool shed, Henry's a coal shovel,

Ginger's a fern trowel and Douglas's a rusty, discarded fish slice that he had discovered in the dust-bin.

"We'd better start on the provisions now jus' to give us strength, hadn't we?" said Douglas when they had dug for some time. "I can feel my strength startin' to go already."

The others agreed and a few moments' steady application disposed of their whole store of provisions.

"Now let's try the drink," said Ginger.

"No," said William firmly. "We've got to keep that. We might need it to save us goin' mad with thirst. Explorers do go mad with thirst an' we might get half-way down the earth an' then start goin' mad with thirst so we've got to keep it till then jus' in case."

They assented with some reluctance and returned to their labours, digging strenuously and—for some time— in silence.

"We're gettin' on jolly well, aren't we?" said Henry at last, pausing to wipe the perspiration and earth from his brow.

All the Outlaws were freely bespattered with earth, for their digging, though spirited, was a little indiscriminate, and shovelfuls of earth rose like fountains in all directions.

"They might make us rulers of it if we find it," panted William.

"What?" said Henry.

"Elizabetha," said William, through a mouthful of soil that he had just received from his own spade. "People that find a new country gen'rally do get made rulers of it. It'd belong to the Queen, of course, but we'd be rulers of it. I've always wanted to be ruler of a country."

"This fish slice has broke," said Douglas. "I'm goin' to use my hands. It's the way prehistoric people mus' have dug an' they were jolly good diggers. You've got to go *miles* under the earth to find their stuff."

"I wish you'd keep your soil to yourself," said Henry, shaking a trowelful of earth from his hair.

"I like that!" said Ginger indignantly. "I've jus' had a whole shovelful of yours down my neck."

"We may have to conquer it," said William. "It may have savages in it."

"Well, let's not start another war," said Douglas. "We've only jus' got bananas back."

"We might come to coal first," said Ginger. "There's coal in the earth."

"We can sell it if we do," said William. "Coal's jolly valu'ble."

It was at this moment that Douglas gave a yell of excitement.

"I've come to somethin' made of wood," he said.

"Prob'ly a bit of tree," said Henry.

"No, it isn't. Look!"

They crowded round, examining the dark flat surface that Douglas's "digging" had exposed.

"Come on!" said William. "Let's see how far it goes."

They dug with concentrated energy. The wooden surface stretched for one yard . . . two yards. . . .

"It's jolly rotten here," said William. "It's rotten right through. I'm goin' to give it a good bash."

He crashed his spade down on to the rotten wood, and it gave way, falling with an echoing sound into a dim, hollow aperture.

"GOSH!" BREATHED WILLIAM, AS A COLLECTION OF
TARNISHED SILVER ARTICLES ROLLED OUT OF THE
BOX.

"It's a sort of underground room," said William,
peering into the recesses. "I'm goin' down into it to
see what it is."

He knocked away some more of the rotten wood and
let himself down, dropping six or seven feet on to a
cemented floor.

"Are you all right, William?" called Ginger anxiously.

"Yes," said William, picking himself up, "an' it *is* a sort of underground room. There's a box in it. Come on down quick an' have a look. "

They scrambled down as best they could, holding on to the rotten wood and letting themselves go, rolling on to the floor and arising bruised but undaunted.

The "room" had a cement floor and a wooden ceiling supported on wooden pillars. The sides were shored up by rotting wood. At the further end a small flight of wooden steps led up to the ceiling.

Ginger went to them and scrambled up, pushing at the wooden ceiling above his head.

"There's a sort of trap-door here, William," he said, "but I can't open it."

"'Course you can't," said Henry. "It mus' be underneath all those ruins."

William was kneeling beside a large wooden box.

"There's somethin' in it," he said. "It's jolly heavy . . . but it's locked."

Ginger came down from the steps and joined the group.

"It looks rotten," he said. "Let's give it a bash."

William's spade had fallen with them into the room; so, taking it up, they hacked in turn at the side of the box till enough was displaced to enable them to break the rest away.

"Gosh!" breathed William.

For out there rolled a collection of tarnished silver—candlesticks, salvers, jugs, dishes, teapot, knives, forks and spoons.

"Treasure!" they gasped.

"But we don't know it's foreign," said Ginger. "It's got to be foreign for New Elizabethans."

Henry had taken out a grubby handkerchief and was rubbing vigorously at a silver jug.

His efforts revealed a crest, which he examined with interest.

"It's got a sort of picture on," he said.

The crest represented a rearing horse with a spear implanted in its breast, but it was so tarnished as to be almost indecipherable.

"Well, it's a foreign animal, anyway," said William. "It's got a sort of horn coming out of its middle. It's not English."

"An' there's some writin' underneath it," said Henry. He rubbed at the lettering with his handkerchief. "It's—it's 'Fide et Amore'."

"Well, *that's* foreign, anyway," said William triumphantly. "So we've found it. Foreign treasure to give to the country. Now we're New Elizabethans, all right. We won't bother discoverin' that undiscovered country any more. It'd take too long an' this is what we really want to do. We'll take it to the Mayor now, shall we?"

"How'll we get it up?" said Douglas.

"Oh, we'll get it up all right," said William.

And they got it up all right.

They hoisted Ginger up first and handed the pieces to him one by one. William scrambled up last, using the wooden box as a sort of springboard, dragged up the last lap by the hands of his fellow Outlaws. Then, covered with dirt and dust, they proudly surveyed the treasure trove.

WILLIAM AND GINGER, FESTOONED WITH RED, WHITE AND
BLUE, TRUNDLED THE BARROW, WHILE HENRY AND
DOUGLAS MARCHED IN FRONT CARRYING FLAGS.

"I bet that ole Drake didn't find anythin' as good as
this," said William.

"How're we goin' to get it to the Mayor?" said
Douglas.

"In the wheelbarrow," said William, "an' we'll do
it prop'ly. I bet Drake did it prop'ly. We'll all go
home an' fetch the dec'rations we had for Coronation
an' we'll dec'rate the wheelbarrow. We can't jus'
take it anyway as if we weren't New Elizabethans."

They concealed the treasure in a bush and went home,

returning with the spoils of their Coronation Day
decorations—streamers, festoons, rosettes, Union Jacks,
bunting and a large coloured picture of the Queen
—which had fortunately been stored in easily access-
ible places. The silver was placed in the wheelbarrow, and streamers, festoons, rosettes, bunting and
Union Jacks were pinned about it (Henry had thoughtfully brought a box of drawing-pins). The picture of
the Queen was balanced on the top, propped up against
a large silver teapot. Henry and Douglas marched in
front, carrying Union Jacks over their shoulders, and
behind them William and Ginger, their persons
festooned in red, white and blue, trundled the barrow.

"I bet this is how Drake did it," said William,
proudly surveying the procession.

They made their colourful progress down the village
street. Passers-by looked at them with amused curiosity, but no one stopped them or questioned them.

They slackened their pace as they neared Mr.
Kirkham's house.

"I bet he'll be surprised," said William. "I bet this treasure's jus' about the las' thing he's thinkin' of."

But William was wrong.

Mr. Kirkham was not only thinking of the treasure but actually discussing it with a friend whom he had asked in to drink a glass of sherry with him before dinner. The guest had just admired the collection of miniatures that hung over the chimney-piece.

"Yes, they're one of my few family heirlooms," said Mr. Kirkham. He was a tall man with a wide mouth and kindly humorous eyes. "We had some very fine silver in the family, but it all went when my uncle's home was bombed. Grantham Lodge, you know."

"Do you mean that the silver was actually bombed?" said the guest.

"No, it just vanished. There were some pretty dubious evacuees about the place and there was a good deal of looting. Anyway, we never found a trace of it. . . . The old chap had a stroke, you know, the day of the bombing and died the next week without recovering consciousness."

"He was a very eccentric character, wasn't he?"

"Most eccentric. He'd taken a dislike to me and wouldn't let me into the place, so I don't even know where he kept the silver, I know that he treasured it tremendously and was terrified of its being destroyed. I thought at first that he might have put it in a safe in the bank, but, as I said, no trace of it has ever been found. He was a curious old chap—very suspicious and secretive. He'd have cut me out of his will if he'd remembered to make one, but——"

"Good Lord!" interrupted the guest, who was sitting near the window. "There's a most peculiar equipage coming up your drive."

Mr. Kirkham went to the window and looked at the laden wheelbarrow, fluttering with flags and bunting, and the four grubby small boys with set, earnest faces who accompanied it.

"What on earth——!" said Mr. Kirkham.

He went to the front door and opened it.

"Who are you and what's all this?" he demanded.

"We're New Elizabethans," said William, "an' this is foreign treasure for the country. Can we bring it in?"

"By all means," said Mr. Kirkham, standing aside. William wheeled the barrow into the room and removed the Queen's picture.

"Good Heavens!" gasped Mr. Kirkham. "The family silver!"

"It's foreign," said William. "It's foreign treasure for the country. Same as Drake."

"Suppose you tell me all about it," said Mr. Kirkham. William told him all about it.

"Of course, that's the explanation," said Mr. Kirkham to his guest. "The old chap got this underground hide-out made, and the place was bombed as soon as he'd moved the silver into it. The steps and the trap-door probably led into the library, but that's still covered with rubble."

"Well, the mystery's solved at last," said the guest, "and you've got your family silver back."

William's face had fallen.

"D'you mean it's not foreign treasure, after all," he said, "an' we can't give it to the country?"

Mr. Kirkham looked at the silver thoughtfully.

"Do you know," he said in a tone of mild surprise, "I find I don't really want the stuff. I've got on very happily all these years without it and it will only add to the complications of life." He turned to William. "I'll tell you what I'll do. There may be some legal formalities to go through first, but when I've gone through them I'll sell it and I'll make out a list of things we could do with the money that would definitely help the country and you shall choose the one you like best."

"Couldn't we send her the money in stamps for the country?" said William, looking at the picture of the Queen that was now propped against the end of the wheelbarrow. "You can send money in stamps."

"I think not," said Mr. Kirkham, "but I promise to find some way of using the money that you'll approve of."

"An'—we'll have found foreign treasure an' given it to the country?"

"Exactly," said Mr. Kirkham.

"Same as Drake?"

"More or less."

"An' we're New Elizabethans?"

"Very much so."

William drew a deep breath of satisfaction.

"We ought to have a drink on that," said the guest.

"I've got a drink," said William, delving beneath the flags and bunting and bringing out his bottle. "I mixed it myself. It's jolly good. Shall I try it first, then you'll know it's all right?"

"Please," said Mr. Kirkham.

William stood erect, raised the bottle to the picture of the Queen, and took a deep draught.

"Your turn next," he said, wiping his mouth on the back of his hand and giving the bottle to Mr. Kirkham.

Mr. Kirkham also raised the bottle to the picture of his Sovereign and took a draught. He flinched, but—by a supreme effort of self-control—not too noticeably.

The guest followed suit, less successful, despite his efforts, at controlling a shudder of revulsion.

Henry, Ginger and Douglas, who were more accustomed to William's mixed drinks, drank in their turn with obvious relish.

"Well, that's all fixed up," said William.

The adventure was over and now belonged to the past. His eyes roved round the room, brightening as they lit on a dart board that leant against the side of a book-case.

"Gosh!" he said. "Is that a dart board?"

"Yes," said Mr. Kirkham. "Like a game?"

"Yes, please," said William eagerly.

The Outlaws gathered round to join in the game. It proceeded with growing enthusiasm as darts embedded themselves in the wall, in the upholstery, in the carpet, in the curtains. . . .

Suddenly Ginger gave a shout.

"I say, William, Hubert Lane's back! He's jus' passing the gate with his gang. Let's go out after him quick!"

William turned, a dart poised in his hand. His mouth widened to a grin.

"There's time to finish the game an' beat the Laneites, too," he said.

CHAPTER VII

WILLIAM AND THE OVER-TEN CLUB

"NOW hurry up with your breakfast, William,"
said Mrs. Brown, "and do try to eat properly."
There was a wistful note in her voice. Usually she
looked forward to a few minutes' peace after Mr.
Brown's whirlwind departure for the station to catch
his morning train, but William's school holidays had
begun and it was difficult to reconcile William's presence with an atmosphere of peace.

"And Mrs. Peters isn't coming this morning," she
added, "so I shall have a lot to do."

William, his brows drawn into a purposeful frown,
continued to pour milk into the moat of a porridge
fortress that sagged in the middle of his plate.

"This porridge isn't thick enough," he complained.
"I can't make any battlements. 'Least, they keep
floppin' over. An' I can't get the drawbridge to stand
up prop'ly either . . . Why isn't she comin'?"

"Because she's going on a charabanc ride to the sea
with the Over-Sixty Club. Do stop messing about with
your food, William."

"I'm not messin'. . . . The moat's overflowed its
banks. Well, I bet that'll keep enemies off all right
even if the drawbridge *has* splodged right down in the
middle of it. I'll pretend a tank's gone over it an'
crashed right through it, hurtling to its doom in the

178

raging torrent below. . . . Can I have a piece of sugar for the tank, please?"

"No, William. Eat your porridge if you want it and leave it if you don't."

"I do want it. I'm goin' to eat it now. This spoon's a jet bomber swoopin' down on the fortress." He emitted a nerve-shattering sound, then looked earnestly at his mother. "Did that sound like a jet bomber?"

"I don't know," said Mrs. Brown faintly, "but don't do it again."

"All right," said William and continued, in a voice muffled by two battlements and a drawbridge, "Gosh! An' she went to the pictures with 'em las' Monday an' she went out to tea with 'em the Monday before."

"Yes, Sir Gerald and Lady Markham kindly asked them all to tea at Marleigh Manor . . . Now, William, have you finished?"

"Nearly."

William disposed of the remainder of the porridge with an abstracted air, obviously no longer interested in the aerial assault.

"Gosh!" he said as he laid down his spoon. "They get everythin' done for them."

"Who gets everything done for them? Here's a sausage for you if you want it."

"Thanks. Why do they always make sausages the same shape? If I made 'em I'd make 'em all diff'rent shapes. I'd make some like ships an' some like trains an' some like aeroplanes an' some like——"

"Do hurry, William. I want to start the washing-up."

"All right. I'll hurry now. . . . The old."

"What on earth are you talking about, dear?"

"The old," repeated William sombrely. "They get everythin' done for them. Old Age Pensions an' Over-Sixty Clubs an' everythin'. It isn't fair. I tried to get Young Age Pensions fixed up once but no one'd listen to me. Why shouldn't we have Young Age Pensions same as they have Old Age Pensions? It jus' isn't fair."

"Don't be so silly, dear, and fold up your table napkin if you've finished."

"They jus' get paid for bein' old. Well, what I say is, why shun't we get paid for bein' young, same as they get paid for bein' old? What's the diff'rence?"

"I said *fold* it, William, not screw it into creases like that. People naturally want to do all they can to cheer up the old."

"Well, why don't they want to do all they can to cheer up the young?" said William, shaking out his table napkin and screwing it into a fresh assortment of creases. "I bet the young need cheerin' up a jolly sight more than what the old do. The old don't have to go to school every day, wearin' out their brains with mental torcher over Latin an' sums an' things. I wrote to the gov'n'ment about Young Age Pensions but they never answered. An' now this Over-Sixty Club! Goin' off to the seaside an' pictures an' tea parties! They jus' get *everythin'* done for them. . . . Can I scrape out the honey, please? It's nearly finished."

"There's quite a lot left in it, William. . . . Oh, very well. And you can give me a hand with putting the things on the trolley, if you like."

"Yes, I will," said William through a mouthful of honey. "Why don't we keep bees? I'd look after

'em. They eat flowers an' there's lots of flowers about,
so they wouldn't cost anythin' to feed. Not like dog
biscuits an' ants' eggs. An' I bet I could teach them
tricks." He stacked up a pile of plates and saucers,
adding a leaning tower of cups which was only saved
from collapse by Mrs. Brown's presence of mind.

"William! Do be more careful. Put the things on
the trolley one by one. . . . Of course we can't keep
bees and it's only natural that people should want to
help the old and be careful with that sugar basin.
You'll have it all over the trolley waving it about like
that. There! I knew you would! If you're going to
help, do try to give your mind to it."

William tried to give his mind to it, but his thoughts
were still busy with his grievances.

"Jus' think of those old Over-Sixty people goin'
swimmin' in the sea while we're doin' rotten old sums
an' g'ography! Can I wheel the trolley into the
kitchen now?"

"I don't suppose that any of them go swimming in
the sea," said Mrs. Brown, recoiling from a mental
picture of her "daily help" in swimming costume,
"and be careful with the trolley . . . There! I knew
you were going to bang it into the kitchen table."

"Sorry. There's only a bit of milk gone on the
floor. I'll wipe it up."

"Not with the tea-towel, William!"

"All right! I'll use this duster."

"That's *not* a duster, William. It's a tray-cloth."

"Sorry . . . Listen! Who started all these Over-
Sixty Clubs an' things, anyway?"

"I suppose someone just thought of it and did
it. Now, William, don't put the loaf in the fridge."

"Sorry . . . I was thinkin' of somethin' else. . . . I s'pose anyone can start clubs anywhere?"

"I suppose so. Look! I knew you were going to spill that honey. Now it's all over the dresser."

"'S all right. I can lick it off. . . . Shall I wash up for you now?"

"No, thank you, dear."

"But I want to help you now Mrs. Peters has gone off swimmin' in the sea."

"No, thank you, dear," said Mrs. Brown, adding hopefully: "Isn't there anything you'd rather be doing somewhere else?"

"Well, axshully, there is," said William, "an' I *have* helped, haven't I?"

"Yes, dear."

"Well, I'll go now if you're sure you can manage without me."

"I'm quite sure, dear."

"All right. I'll go an' find Ginger an' Henry an' Douglas."

He plunged upstairs to his bedroom and returned, sliding down the banisters and landing noisily on the floor at the bottom. His untuneful whistle dispelled from the countryside the last lingering traces of its early morning hush as he set off down the road.

Mrs. Brown threw a harassed glance at the sugar on the trolley, the milk on the floor, the honey on the dresser, and the trail of small oddments of cutlery that marked the passage of the trolley from dining-room to kitchen . . . then set herself briskly to the work of clearing up.

William had collected Ginger, Henry and Douglas

and was holding forth to them eloquently as they made their way towards the old barn.

"They get money an' rides to the seaside an' pictures an' theatres an' tea parties an'—an' everythin' *given* to 'em jus' 'cause they're old. Think of 'em all swimmin' in the sea an' we've not been to the seaside since—since—well, since the las' time we went. It's not fair an' somethin' ought to be done about it."

"What *can* be done about it?" said Ginger, retrieving from the ditch a fragment of a branch that had been blown down in a recent gale and flourishing it in the manner of a walking stick.

"Well, I'm tired of writing to the gov'n'ment," said William. "I've never had an answer yet. Huh!" He gave his short sarcastic laugh. "Seems to me this old Minister of Old Age Pensions, whoever he is, has got so old he's forgot how to write. Anyway, when we get a Minister of Young Age Pensions——"

"I bet we never will," said Douglas gloomily. "I bet the Black Rod or the Head of the Opposition or someone'll stop us."

"'Course we'll get one," said William. "I'll be him myself when I'm grown up, an' then I'll get things goin' a bit better than what they are now."

"I don't see how you're goin' to find time for all the things you're goin' to be," said Henry, "inventor, an' air pilot an' diver an' fireman an' sweet-shop man an' engine-driver an' now Minister of Young Age Pensions."

"Oh, I'll get 'em in all right," said William airily. "They're all jolly easy things to do once you get into the way of them."

"An' if we've got to wait till you're grown up before

"YOU'RE ONLY NINE, ARABELLA SIMPKIN," SAID WILLIAM
STERNLY, "SO YOU CAN JOLLY WELL CLEAR OUT."

we get anythin' done, it won't be much good to us,"
said Douglas.

"Well, we won't have to wait," said William.
"We'll have to wait for Young Age Pensions, of course,
but we needn't wait for things like Over-Sixty Clubs.
We could start that straight away."

"What's the use of an Over-Sixty Club to us?" said
Douglas.   "It'll be years an' years before we get to
be over sixty."

"Don't be such a chump," said William.   "We
wouldn't have it over sixty.   We'd have it our age.
We'd have——" He paused to consider.   "We'd

have—— Yes, we'd have an Over-Ten Club. We're all over ten, so we could have an Over-Ten Club easy. Then we could have a jolly good time goin' to pictures an' theatres an' tea parties an' havin' charabanc rides to the sea."

"Yes, but how are we goin' to *get* 'em—pictures an' tea parties an' things?" said Henry, who was of a practical turn of mind.

"Oh, we won't bother about that jus' yet," said William, waving the question aside impatiently. "*They* get 'em so I don't see why we shouldn't. I bet it's quite easy to fix up. The first thing to do is to get this Over-Ten Club started."

"An' how're you goin' to do it?" said Ginger, leaning heavily upon his stick and falling to the ground as it collapsed beneath his weight. "I bet it's not as easy as all that, startin' clubs."

"'Course it is," said William, giving Ginger's mishap the tribute of a derisive chuckle. "We'll put up a notice on the door of the old barn. I bet people'll join all right when we tell 'em all the excitin' things they're goin' to do."

"Yes, it's not the joinin' part that's worryin' me," said Ginger, brushing himself down and throwing away the remnants of his stick. "Must have had dry rot in it or this death clock beetle what churches get. It looked all right . . . What's worryin' me is what's goin' to happen after they've joined."

"If everyone was like you," said William severely, "no one'd ever have discovered anythin'—not America nor—nor fountain pens nor anythin'."

"I think it's goin' to be a waste of time," said Douglas. "I'd rather be playin' Lions an' Tamers."

"Yes, it's a good game, is Lions an' Tamers," said William reflectively, adding: "P'raps we could work it into the Over-Ten Club, once we get it goin'."

"Lions and Tamers" was strongly disapproved of by the Outlaws' mothers but it was a game that the Outlaws had played ever since they could remember. Although there were long periods when it sank into disuse, they would revive it at regular intervals, playing it in season and out of season with such abandon that it was generally forbidden again by Authority before they had had time to tire of it. It was essentially a simple game without complicated rules—indeed without any rules at all. Half the players were lions and half were tamers. The tamers tried to tame the lions and the lions resisted the tamers' efforts with all the ferocity they could muster. It was a game with no formal beginning and no formal end. The players began it when their high spirits felt the need of immediate outlet and stopped when they were too much exhausted to continue.

"But we've gotter get the club goin' first," said William. "Come on. Let's write out the notice for the meetin' an' see how many of 'em turn up."

The notice was composed by William, written by Ginger and edited by Douglas, who altered the spelling of "president" from "pressidunt" to "prezidant" and put in an occasional comma. In order to give it an official air, Henry had printed the words "Countie Burrow of Hadley" in red ink at the top and affixed a three-halfpenny stamp taken from the envelope of a circular that he had found in the waste-paper basket at home.

It read:

Nottis Ergunt.

overtenn klub

Their will, be a meating tomorrough afternun of
peeple over, tenn to gett up an overtenn, klub
ennyone, overtenn kan kum not, annimuls William
Brown prezidant will maik a speach peeple, that
interrupp him will, be chuckd out

cined William Brown

The attendance at the meeting was gratifying, though
the "over ten" qualification seemed to have been
largely ignored.   As usual the entire juvenile popula-
tion of the village flocked to the old barn, headed by
Arabella Simpkin, wheeling her baby brother in a ramshackle pram, and wearing a moth-eaten fur and a
ragged eye-veil (both belonging to her mother) in order
to lend her an air of maturity.

"You're only nine, Arabella Simpkin," said William
sternly.   "So you can jolly well clear out."

"You shut up, William Brown," said Arabella
Simpkin haughtily.   "Always poking your nose into
things what aren't your business."

"It *is* my business," said William,   "I'm gettin' up
this club an' it's for over-ten people, not for kids like
you."

Arabella gave a shrill laugh.

"D'you think I *want* to b'long to your rotten ole
club, William Brown?   Huh!   Fancy you thinkin' I
want to b'long to your rotten ole club!"

"All right, go home then," said William.   "You're
nine an' we don't want kids of nine."

Arabella repeated the shrill laugh.

"Fancy you thinkin' I'm only nine, William Brown! You *are* ig'rant."

"How old are you, then?" challenged William.

"I'm—I'm sixteen," said Arabella defiantly, tossing the string of moth-eaten fur about her neck and fingering the eye-veil with such a fierce gesture that it slipped its moorings on her school beret and came down over her mouth.

There was a murmur of expostulation.

"Oo, you story teller!"

"Oo, you're nine.   I *know* you're nine."

"She was eight las' year an' seven the year before, so she *mus'* be nine.   Oo, isn't she a story teller?"

Realising that the feeling of the assembly was against her on this point, Arabella shifted her attack to more general grounds.

"Who d'you think you are, William Brown, bossing people round?   King of the Cannibal Isles, I shouldn't wonder!"

"Chuck her out!" said Henry.

"Yes, you try!" shrilled Arabella, standing arms akimbo and sucking her eye-veil furiously.   "Jus' you *try* chuckin' me out!"

"Well, look at him," said William, pointing to the baby and shifting his line of attack in his turn.   "What's he doin' here, anyway?   You can't say *he's* over ten."

The baby stared at William dispassionately for a few moments then bent his whole attention to the work of blowing bubbles with his saliva.

"He's two," chorused the meeting.   "We know he's two 'cause his mother says so.   An' Arabella's nine 'cause we *know* she is."

G

A smile of triumph curved Arabella's thin lips.

"Well, that makes us a person of eleven between us, doesn't it? so we *can* b'long. We can b'long as a person of eleven, so *there*, William Brown!"

"Gosh! You can't do that," said William, taken aback.

"There's nothin' in the notice to say you can't," said Arabella, "an' I'm goin' to. We're a person of eleven —our Fred an' me—an' you can't stop us joinin' your ole club, so there!"

William would have liked to continue the argument but the meeting was growing restive.

"Well, come on," said a small stocky child with beetling brows and a mouth that showed determination, despite the liquorice bootlace that dangled from it. "Is anythin' goin' to happen or isn't it?"

"Yes, it is, if you'll all shut up a minute," said William, mounting the packing case that served him as a platform. "If you'll all shut up a minute an' listen I'm goin' to make a speech."

A ragged cheer of mingled applause and derision arose.

"Now listen to me," said William, raising his voice above the uproar. "Kin'ly listen to me. I'm goin' to start makin' this speech. Ladies an' gentlemen——"

Another ragged cheer arose, through which Arabella's voice could be heard saying with shrill sarcasm: "I mus' be blind. I don't see no gentlemen."

"Shut up, Arabella Simpkin," said William. "Now listen to me, everybody. I'm the president an' I'm makin' this speech. Now listen." The murmurs died away. "There's a club called the Over-Sixty Club what people over sixty belong to an' they have a jolly good time jus' 'cause they're over sixty, an' what I say is I don't see why we shouldn't have a jolly good time jus' 'cause we're over ten. There's lors that people shouldn't be punished for things that aren't their fault an' it's not our fault we're not over sixty an' even if we *tried* to be over sixty we couldn't 'cause you can't be over sixty if you're not over sixty by nacher so it's not fair an' something ought to be done about it."

A confused babble arose as the audience awoke to a sense of its grievances.

"Let's go an' give 'em a bashin'," said a small angelic-looking boy with large blue eyes and blond hair.

"Let's dress up as over sixty with beards an' things," said Frankie Parker. "I could borrow my grand-mother's ear trumpet. She'd jus' think she'd lost it. She's always losin' it."

"There's a ninvalid chair in our garage what my great uncle used to drive, but I dunno how to drive it."

"There's two walking sticks at home. I could use 'em, same as crutches."

"Why not wait till we get to be over sixty?" suggested a placid-looking child who was licking a toffee apple. "Everyone gets to be over sixty if they wait long enough. It only wants a bit of patience."

"I'd like to see William Brown sixty," jeered Arabella. "Gosh! He'll be worth lookin' at. He's a sight to start with."

"Shut up, Arabella Simpkin," said William. "Shut up, everyone. Now listen to me, all of you. I'm goin' to go on makin' this speech. Shut up an' listen to me goin' on makin' this speech." The uproar died away again to a few murmurings. "I'm goin' to start it

again from the beginnin'. Ladies an' gentlemen, those
old over-sixties get everythin' done for them an' I bet
it's time we had somethin' done for us an' I'm goin' to
start an Over-Ten club an' all of you that's over ten
can b'long an' we'll have tea parties an' cinemas an'
rides to the sea-side same as what they do." A loud
cheer arose. "Anyone what wants to join put their
hands up."

A forest of hands arose.

"They can't all join," said Henry. "Some of 'em
are jus' children. I bet that more'n half of them
aren't over ten."

"Well, it's no good tryin' to sort 'em out," said
Douglas. "We'd only get in a muddle."

"We'll sort 'em out later," said William. "We've
got to get it fixed up prop'ly first."

But the club seemed to consider itself fixed up
properly already. They swarmed round William
eagerly, expectantly, with a touching trust and
confidence.

"Come on, William!"

"What'll we do first, William?"

"Let's go to the pictures."

"Let's go to the seaside."

"No, let's have a tea party, William."

William was a little disconcerted by the immediate
success of his scheme.

"We can't do anythin' straight away," he temporised.
"We—well, we've got to think things out a bit first.
I dunno that we can do anythin' jus' now. Not jus'
this minute. I mean—well, I mean——"

They interrupted him with indignant protests.

"You *said* we could go to the pictures."

"You *promised* we could go to the seaside."

"I want to go *now!*"

"Huh!" jeered Arabella. "Might've known William Brown couldn't do nothin' but make speeches. Not much of a speech neither, he didn't make. Our Fred here could make a better speech than what he did, any day."

As if to prove this point, Fred raised his voice in a prolonged howl. Through the howl the protests continued.

"Calling himself King of the Cannibal Isles an' can't even take people to the seaside."

"I never did," said William.

"Where's this tea party you kept talkin' about?"

"Oh, he can *talk* all right," said Arabella. "He can make as much noise as a donkey but he can't *do* nothin'. That's him all over."

"You *can* do somethin', can't you, William?"

"Reg'lar swindle, that's what it is," said Arabella, tossing the moth-eaten fur over her shoulder with such *élan* that it landed on the ground a few yards behind her. "Oughter be in prison, that's where he ought to be."

"You *can* take us somewhere, can't you, William?"

"'Course I can," said William. "'*Course* I can, an' you can jolly well shut up, Arabella Simpkin. What d'you think I started this club for if I couldn't? Come on!"

Cheers greeted this pronouncement and, before William quite knew what was happening, he found himself walking across the fields towards Hadley, his Over-Ten Club clamouring excitedly at his heels.

"The pictures!"

"Let's go to the pictures."

"Gosh! Isn't it smashing! William's takin' us to the pictures."

William's faint disclaimers were drowned in the uproar and in less than a minute, as it seemed to him, he was being propelled along Hadley's main street towards Hadley's main cinema.

At the door he turned to survey the rag, tag and bobtail that comprised his Over-Ten Club. Fortunately the disgrace of the pram had been removed. (Arabella's mother had indignantly retrieved it on its reckless passage through the village), but Arabella still headed the crowd, her fur perched precariously on her shoulder, her eye-veil dangling in a drunken fashion from one corner of her school beret.

"You'd better wait out here while I go in an' fix it up," said William in a tone of authority that did not quite conceal an underlying nervousness. "Count 'em, Ginger. How many of them are there?"

"About nineteen, I think," said Ginger. "I can't count 'em all 'cause they keep movin' about."

A small boy was running excitedly in and out of the others and a little girl was hopping up and down the steps that led to the entrance, singing "Polly Wolly Doodle," in a shrill tuneless voice. The commissionaire eyed them with mingled apprehension and distaste.

"Well, go on, William Brown," said Arabella. "How much longer are you goin' to keep us hangin' round?"

"All right, all right," said William. "I've gotter have time to breathe, haven't I, same as everyone else."

He mounted the steps and approached the pay desk in a nonchalant fashion.

"Nineteen one-an'-sixpennies," he said to the man at the desk.

The man at the desk stared at him.

"Where's your money?" he said.

"I haven't any," said William. "We don't pay. We're the Over-Ten Club."

"The—*what*?" said the man.

"The Over-Ten Club," explained William patiently. "Same as the Over-Sixty Club. We go into things free."

"You——?" For a moment the man's indignation deprived him of speech. Then it returned. "Out you go, my lad, and quicker than you came in and if I have any more of your monkey tricks——"

There was something in his tone that made William turn hurriedly towards the exit. His Over-Ten Club closed round him eagerly.

"Is it all right, William?"

"Can we go in now, William?"

"No," said William. "No, it's—it's not a good film. You wouldn't like it. I had a good look at the pictures of it an'—well, it's a jolly dull film. You wouldn't like it. I said we wouldn't go to it, 'cause it's such a jolly dull film."

There was a murmur of disappointment.

"I wouldn't mind," said the stocky little girl with beetling brows. "I like dull films."

The commissionaire was bearing down threateningly upon them and William set off hastily along the street, followed by his motley crew.

"What are we goin' to do, William?"

"Let's go to the seaside, shall we, William?"

"Look!" shrilled Arabella, pointing with a small claw-like hand across the street.

Outside a tobacconist-and-sweetshop stood a large notice.

"Daily outings to Brighton, Worthing, Hastings."

An eager clamour arose from the Over-Ten Club.

"The seaside!"

"Look, William, we can go to the seaside now."

"Come on quick! Let's go to the seaside."

"Well—er—you'd better wait here, while I fix it up," said William, goaded into action despite his misgivings. "You wait here while I go across an' fix it up."

"Yes, same as you did las' time," taunted Arabella. "You fixed it up jolly well las' time, didn't you! I s'pose you'll be sayin' it's a dull seaside or somethin' like that. Trust you to make a mess of it, William Brown."

"You wait!" said William. "You jus' wait an' see. I'll go across now an' I bet it'll be all right."

He crossed the street and entered the shop. A bored-looking youth with long hair and a receding chin came forward.

"We—er—we want to go to the seaside," said William.

Surprise invaded the boredom of the young man's face.

"We?" he said.

"Yes," said William. "About twenty of us."

"You mean—you wish to charter a charabanc?"

"Yes," said William.

"When do you wish to go?"

"Now," said William.

Suspicion struggled with surprise in the young man's face.

"I could fix you up tomorrow . . ."

"All right," said William. "Tomorrow'd do. We can put it off till tomorrow all right."

"You'll pay a deposit, I take it?"

"No," said William, "we don't pay anythin.' We go free. We're the Over Ten-Club. Same as the Over-Sixty Club, you know."

His friends watched his summary ejection from the shop with mild surprise. He had regained something of his aplomb, however, when he rejoined them.

"You came out jolly quick," said Ginger.

"Yes," said William. "I was in a bit of a hurry an' I didn't want to waste any more time talkin' to him."

"What about goin' to the seaside, William?"

"Can we start now, William?"

"Can I catch a crab, William?"

"Can I jus' run home to fetch my bucket an' spade, William?"

"Well, you see," said William, "I'm sorry about it, but it's—it's jolly cold at the seaside jus' now. You wouldn't enjoy it. 'S no good goin' to things you wouldn't enjoy. So I told him we wouldn't go . . . 'S no good goin' if it's cold. I b'lieve it's rainin' at the seaside, as well. Snowin', too, I shouldn't wonder."

Their excitement changed again to disappointment.

"What can we do, then, William?"

"What about that tea party, William? Will you take us to that tea party, if we can't go to the pictures or the seaside?"

"Er—yes," said William. He felt as if he were in the grip of one of those nightmares from which one longs unavailingly to awake. "Oh, yes, a little thing like a party's nothin' to me. Huh!"

They straggled on down the street.

"OH, HERE YOU ARE, CHILDREN," SAID THE HARASSED-
LOOKING WOMAN AS WILLIAM AND HIS BAND APPEARED.
"COME ALONG IN."

"I dunno . . ." said William hoarsely. "I mean . . .
I wonder . . . I mean, p'raps we'd better put it off a
bit till I've got somethin' better fixed up."

Resentful murmurs arose.

"I want a tea party if I can't go to the seaside."

"You *promised* us a tea party, William."

"I'd have *liked* that dull film, William."

"I wouldn't have minded if it *was* snowin' at the seaside, William."

"I'm getting ever so hungry, William.   Where *is* this tea party?"

"Will there be chocolate biscuits, William?"

"Are we nearly there, William?"

Arabella's voice rose shrilly over the murmurs.

"I b'lieve there ain't no tea party, neither.   Huh! It'll be snowin' at the tea party same as at the seaside. He'll get out of it somehow.   A reg'lar swindler, he is. He ought to be shut up in the Tower same as the ones in hist'ry."

"Jus' you *wait*," said the goaded William.   "Jus' you wait till you get to this party.   You'll be jolly well surprised when you get to it."

"Yes, we'll be s'prised if anythin' happens. . . ."

But just then something did happen. They were passing a large building at the door of which stood a small harassed-looking woman. Her face broke into smiles of welcome as her eyes lit on William and his band.

"Oh, there you are, children! We were so afraid you wouldn't be able to get here. Come along in."

The children swarmed into the room. At one end several elderly people sat dejectedly round little tables. At the other end a large trestle table was laden with cakes, jellies, chocolate biscuits and other dainties.

"I'm Miss Fountain, children," said the lady, "and when Miss Mirabel rang up this morning to say that the fog was so thick in London that she didn't think you'd be able to come I was terribly disappointed, but I still clung to the hope that it would clear and that you'd come, after all, and, you see"—she laughed gaily —"I was right. I had one of my *feelings* that you'd come and they very seldom mislead me. Come along. . . . I knew that you'd be hungry after your journey, so I thought I'd give you a nice tea before you began your dancing. I've been reading extracts from Tennyson aloud to our Over-Sixties and, though I'm sure they've enjoyed it, no doubt they'll be glad of a change. . . . Miss Mirabel's not come with you, I see."

"No," said William, feeling that some answer was expected.

"Oh, well, I suppose you know what to do. She said that it was a particularly busy week for her. What about your costumes? Have you brought them with you?"

"No," said William.

"Oh, dear!   She said that a friend would be bringing them separately in her car, but no doubt the fog has delayed things.   I suppose that you can dance just as well without them?"

"Yes," said William, still following the line of least resistance.

The others were not listening to the conversation. They had taken their seats at the table and were already hard at work on the feast.   William made haste to join them and they greeted him with cries of delight.

"Oo, William, it's lovely!"

"It's a *real* tea party."

"Oo, *look* at that pink cake!"

"An' that red jelly."

"Oo, William, it's better than the pictures."

Even Arabella found time to remark grudgingly through a mouthful of jam sandwich: "Well, you've not made a muddle over *this*, William Brown, I mus' say."

Miss Fountain was addressing the depressed-looking gathering at the other end of the room.

"You'll all be glad to know that Miss Mirabel's Juveniles have managed to get here, after all.   Without Miss Mirabel and without their costumes, I'm afraid, but I'm sure you won't mind that.   We'll enjoy their beautiful dancing just as much in everyday clothes. . . .   I won't continue the Tennyson reading in the circumstances——"

A faint cheer arose from her audience and she gave them a gratified smile.

"I'm so glad you enjoyed it.   And now I'll go and see how the Juveniles are getting on."

Neither William nor any of his band had listened to

the speech. They were busy clearing up the remnants of the feast, disposing of the last crumbs of cakes, sandwiches and biscuits, the last shreds of jelly and trifle. Then William noticed that Miss Fountain was hovering anxiously about him.

"You're in charge of the Juveniles, aren't you, dear?" she said.

"Yes," said William.

"Well, perhaps, if you've all finished your tea you'd get them started, would you, dear? I don't know whether you want music, do you, dear?"

"No, thanks," said William. "No, we don't want music."

"Such a good thing, because, though there is a piano and I do play a little, I'm not very sure of the notes and actually only certain of the notes on this particular instrument give out any sound at all, so, as I suppose that Miss Mirabel generally plays for you and as she couldn't come with you, perhaps it would be best to dispense with music altogether." Being an optimistic woman, she mistook William's stare of blank bewilderment for a look of intelligence and continued: "Well, you'll see to it all, won't you, dear? We've left a good clear space for you."

She went to the other end of the room and took her place among the Over-Sixties, watching William and his Over-Tens with an expectant smile.

"Well, we've had a jolly good tea," said Arabella, still grudgingly approving, as she retrieved the eye-veil (which had lost its moorings in the general excitement and fallen limply into her tea-cup), and fastened it, sodden and shapeless, over her beret with an air of exaggerated elegance. "An' what'll we do now?"

William had ceased wrestling with his bewilderment.
Fate had mysteriously led him to this place, provided
him with a lavish tea and set apart a clear expanse of
floor.

"Let's have a game," he said.

"What game?" they clamoured eagerly.

"Lions an' Tamers," said William.

"Oh, goody, goody!" cried the Over-Tens, leaping
exultantly from their seats. "Show us how to play it,
William."

"Well, you jus' pick sides," said William. "an' then
—well, you'll soon see how it goes."

They soon saw how it went. William and Ginger
picked sides and soon the room was a bedlam of
fighting, shouting, scuffling children. Miss Fountain
watched with a growing air of mystification.

"Not a very pretty dance," she murmured to her
neighbour. "Too modern. No rhythm or harmony.
Not at all what I'd expected."

But the Over-Sixties enjoyed it. It was, at any rate,
better than "Break, Break, Break," or the "Ode on the
Death of the Duke of Wellington." One sprightly old
man with mischievous blue eyes and a long humorous
mouth joined in the game as a tamer. Two old women,
rocking with laughter, concealed a couple of lions behind their chairs while they gathered breath to return
to the fray. A sporting-looking old woman who had
won ten shillings on the Derby last year laid a bet of
sixpence on the final result. The others gave encouragement and advice and cheered both sides indis-
criminately. Miss Fountain sat watching in silence,
the smile growing more fixed and frozen on her
face.

It was Douglas who finally pointed out the time.

"I've got to be goin'," he panted to William. "My mother said I'd got to be home early. I got in a row yesterday for makin' toffee in the coffee machine an' I don't want to get into another today."

"All right. P'raps we'd all better go," said William, pulling his tie round from the back of his neck and drawing his shirt together where the buttons had been torn off.

Fate had so far befriended him, but he knew that Fate was not to be relied on indefinitely. The frozen aspect of Miss Fountain's smile held a warning that could no longer be safely ignored. Better go while the going was good. . . .

"Come on, everybody," he shouted. "'S time to go now."

Towsled, dishevelled, panting, he led them up to Miss Fountain, baring his teeth in the glassy smile that comprised his "company manners."

"Thank you very much, Miss Fountain. We've had a very nice time, thank you, an' we've got to go now. . . . Come on!" he shouted in authoritative tones to his fellow guests. "Come on, quick!"

They trooped to the door in a straggling chattering crowd. Miss Fountain watched them, paralysed by amazement. Then, as if their departure broke some spell, she leapt to her feet.

"One moment!" she called, hurrying to the door. "One moment, children!"

She stood at the doorway, peering up and down the road. Her guests had vanished into the dusk.

It was after lunch the next day that William,

"DID YOU ENJOY THE OVER-SIXTY CLUB MEETING
YESTERDAY, MRS. PETERS?" ASKED MRS. BROWN

wandering into the kitchen, where his mother and Mrs.
Peters were washing-up, heard his mother say:

"And did you enjoy the Over-Sixty Club outing
yesterday, Mrs. Peters?"

Mrs. Peters shook her head gloomily as she plunged
the tumblers recklessly into the washing-up water.

"Naw," she said. "Sittin' in that there charabang
got on me nerves an' there weren't nothin' to do at
the seaside when you got there. Now me friend what
goes to the one over at Hadley 'ad a much better time."

"What did they do there, Mrs. Peters?" asked Mrs.

Brown, rescuing a tablespoon that Mrs. Peters had tipped into the chicken bucket along with the mashed potatoes.

"Well, this friend o' mine, she's a bit deaf an' she can never 'ardly 'ear the notices what's give out, but it seems they 'ad a kids' tea party—pore kids from out London way, likely. They give 'em a good tea an' then they all 'ad games. Me friend didn't join in, bein' a bit stiff in 'er joints, like, but she said it were a nice sort o' change, givin' a tea party to pore kids. She enjoyed jus' watchin' of 'em play, 'specially as that there Miss Fountning what was runnin' it 'ad bin a-readin' of po'ms what me friend couldn't 'ear but what they all said she was lucky not bein' able to."

"Oh, yes," said Mrs. Brown. "Miss Fountain . . . She's coming to tea with me today."

"Gosh!" said William in a voice of horror from the doorway.

"What's the matter, dear?" said Mrs. Brown.

"Oh—er—nothin'," said William.

"She's only just come to live in the neighbourhood and I called on her last week. She's very keen on these Over-Sixty Clubs, so they asked her to help with the one in Hadley and she said that she thought that the various local Over-Sixty Clubs should co-operate more and she's coming to tea with me today to discuss it. . . . Will you be in to tea, William?"

"No, I won't," said William firmly.

"All right, dear," smiled Mrs. Brown. "You needn't sound so determined. You'd like her if you met her. She's very nice."

"Yes, I know she is," said William. "I mean, I bet she is. I mean, I've got to go out somewhere very important this afternoon, a long way off, an' I've got to start very early."

His plans, however, miscarried. He wasted an hour or so in the garden, completing the primeval swamp that he was constructing out of the compost heap and the contents of the rain-tub. Then he went upstairs to his bedroom to remove the traces of this occupation and became absorbed in a book called *The Mystery of the Branded Skeleton* that Henry had lent him the evening before . . . so that by the time he crept slowly and silently down the stairs the visitor had already arrived and was ensconced in an arm-chair that commanded a full view of the open sitting-room door.

William hovered in the hall, waiting his opportunity to slip unseen across the open doorway and make good his escape. Miss Fountain's gentle voice floated out to him.

"Yes, I do feel so strongly that we ought to co-operate more closely over these Over-Sixty clubs, Mrs. Brown. Pool ideas and experiences and so on. . . ."

"Yes, of course," said Mrs. Brown, "but I understand that you have a very flourishing one in Hadley. My charwoman was saying that a friend of hers enjoyed yesterday's meeting very much."

A strange expression came into Miss Fountain's pleasant face.

"Yesterday . . . Yesterday's was a most extraordinary experience, Mrs. Brown, and I should like to tell you about it."

"Yes, do, Miss Fountain. I agree that it would be very useful to pool our experiences, as you say."

"It was a *most* extraordinary experience, Mrs. Brown, and I still don't understand it. You see, all the other helpers were down with 'flu and I was left to carry on alone and—it was foolish, perhaps—but I thought I'd like to make a sort of *occasion* of it and provide a really enjoyable entertainment. I'd seen some charming child dancers—Miss Mirabel's Juveniles—at a little charity show in London. They did some delightful old-world dances in old-world costumes—minuets and that sort of thing—so I engaged them at my own expense and, again rather foolishly, perhaps, provided a really good tea for them, so that they would be fresh and in good spirits for their dancing. But evidently there was a thick fog in London——"

"Yes, my husband said there was," put in Mrs. Brown.

"—and Miss Mirabel rang up to say that she was afraid they wouldn't be able to get here, but I had one of my *feelings* that they'd come, after all, and my feelings very seldom mislead me. Anyway, I hoped for the best and got everything ready and meantime read some of my favourite Tennyson poems to the dear old people, which they much enjoyed, and then——" Her voice faltered.

"Yes?" Mrs. Brown encouraged her.

"Well, they came. Miss Mirabel's Juveniles. About twenty of them. The costumes had apparently gone astray and Miss Mirabel had not been able to accompany them, but they came. They did full justice to the tea and then——,'

Again she stopped

"Then they danc'ed for you, I hope?" said Mrs. Brown.

"Yes, they danced, Mrs. Brown, but it was such an odd dance. Chaotic. Without rhythm or harmony or beauty. I'm always so sorry to see this chaotic element in modern art and I was quite distressed to see that it had invaded even children's dancing. There was that note of *violence* in it that one finds nowadays in all modern art. However, they carried the dance through to the end and then went away—rather hurriedly and abruptly, I thought. But no doubt they had to catch their train to London, so one must not blame them for that. But this morning—well, I simply can't understand it . . ."

Again Miss Fountain's voice died away into a perplexed murmur. Again Mrs. Brown gently encouraged her.

"Yes, Miss Fountain?"

"Well, I had a letter from Miss Mirabel, saying how sorry she was that her Juveniles had not been able to come. The whole thing is most mysterious. I can't make head or tail of it . . . Of course, as I said, I was disappointed in the children. I don't think they were the same lot of children as I saw before. They were so much less—dainty and graceful. The boy who appeared to be in charge of them——"

William, absorbed by this recital, had inadvisedly advanced to a spot from which he could see and hear without obstruction, and it was at this point that Miss Fountain turned to see him standing in the doorway. She blinked and gulped.

"Oh, come in, William," said Mrs. Brown. "This is my son, William, Miss Fountain . . . Well, say 'how d'you do,' William."

William, his face wearing its most wooden expression, advanced into the room and held out a grubby hand.

"How d'you do," he said hoarsely.

Miss Fountain still sat there, blinking and gulping as if in the last stages of suffocation.

"If you'll 'scuse me, I've gotter go now," continued William. "I've gotter go quick."

"But ,William——" began Mrs. Brown, then stopped.

The figure of William could be seen making its way in headlong flight down to the gate and along the road towards Ginger's house. The net of Fate was closing round him. There would be questions . . . explanations . . . retribution . . . and he wanted to retreat in as good order as possible.

He held a brief consultation with Ginger, then the two set off for the old barn, carrying a sheet of paper. In silence they affixed the sheet of paper to the door with a drawing pin, then hastened towards the woods with the air of those bent rather upon postponing some inevitable catastrophe than merely enjoying the countryside.

The notice fluttered disconsolately in the breeze. It read:

Overtenn klub

The overtenn klub will be klozed til furthur nottis.

cined William Brown.

CHAPTER VIII

THESE LITTLE MISTAKES WILL HAPPEN

"I'VE thought of somethin' else I'm goin' to be when I'm grown up," said William.

"Gosh! Not another!" said Ginger in reluctant admiration.

William decided on a new career every few days. Already, in the course of the last week, he had decided to be diver, gold-digger, big-game hunter, tree-lopper, conjurer, atom-bomb maker and snake charmer.

"Well, I don't want to waste all my time on one thing, same as most grown-ups do," he said. "Look at my father, goin' to the office every single day! You'd think he'd get sick of it. I'm goin' to do somethin' diff'rent every day, so I've got to think up a lot of things. There's three hundred an' sixty-five days in a year . . . Gosh, that's a water rat! . . . No, it isn't."

William and Ginger were making their usual erratic progress along the road, stopping occasionally to dive into the ditch or to attempt (generally without success) various acrobatic feats on the gates and fences that bordered their path.

"Well, what's this new thing you've thought of?" said Ginger.

"Rounding up wild ponies," said William. "I saw them doin' it on the pictures an' it looked jolly fine. . . .

There was one black an' white one that was smashin'. It jumped about an'—an'—well, it was *smashin'!* I'd like to've had that one for a pet. I bet if I did the roundin' up for them, they'd let me keep one or two for pets, don't you? This little black an' white one . . . it ran round an' round an' jumped up in the air . . ."

"Same as the one the Wonder Cossacks had last year," said Ginger, "the time they came to Five Acre Meadow for jus' that one night."

"Gosh, yes! They were wizard, weren't they? D'you remember that man that jumped from one horse to another in full flight?"

"Yes . . . an' the one that picked things up from the ground, ridin' at lightnin' speed?"

"Yes, an' the horse that jumped right over another horse . . ."

"An' the time they rode with three of 'em standin' on each other's shoulders . . ."

"An' jumped over things an' landed on their horses' backs again without saddles or reins or anythin' . . ."

"An' did a cavalry charge, stoppin' dead on the word of command . . ."

"Gosh!" they both breathed ecstatically as their minds went back to the glorious evening of the Wonder Cossack display.

"I'm goin' to be a Wonder Cossack, too, when I grow up," said William. "I bet I could train those ponies of mine to do all the things they did . . . an' I'm practisin' bein' an acrobat, so I ought to be all right for it." He attempted a hand-spring in the road, rolled into the ditch and picked himself up, saying with dignity, "I meant to do that."

"P'r'aps they'll come back again this year," said

Ginger, whose mind was still running on the Wonder Cossacks.

"I bet they won't," said William. "Things you want to happen twice never do. . . . Our boiler's never burst since that one time. Gosh! It was wizard! Water all over the place!"

"There was a horse that *danced*," said Ginger. "Do you remember?"

"I should think I *do*," said William. "No, I bet they won't ever come again."

"No, p'r'aps they won't," agreed Ginger with a heavy sigh.

The two trudged on dejectedly, hands in pockets, eyes fixed on the ground.

Suddenly Ginger raised his eyes and gave a gasp.

"*Look!*" he said.

They were passing Five Acre Meadow, and there over the gate was a board with a notice:

WONDER COSSACKS
AMAZING EQUESTRIAN FEATS
BARE-BACKED ACROBATIC RIDERS
THE HUMAN HORSE
THE CHARGE OF THE LIGHT BRIGADE
THE EQUINE WALTZERS
TONIGHT ONLY
ENTRANCE 1s.

A man in overalls was smoothing over the notice with a brush.

"Does it mean—tonight?" said William, hardly able to believe his eyes.

"Yip," said the man. "Didn't know we could fit

it in till this mornin'. Next big date's at Leeds, but we're puttin' in a night here an' a night there jus' as it comes along on the way up. Depends on how much time we've got in hand. Keeps us in practice an' in funds an' gives the natives a treat, so there you are!"

With that he slapped his brush into his bucket of paste and strode off.

"We've jus' *got* to go to it, Ginger," said William, adding thoughtfully, "Have you got a shillin'?"

"No," said Ginger. "I haven't got any money at all. Have you?"

"No," said William.

"Would your father give you some?"

"Dunno. He's stopped my pocket money 'cause of a rotten ole window that got in the way of my ball. Would yours?"

"Dunno. Mine's stopped mine 'cause of a rotten ole flower-bed that got in the way of my bike."

"We could try 'em anyway, couldn't we?"

"All right. Let's go back an' try 'em now. It's Saturday so they'll be at home for lunch."

William found Mr. Brown ensconced in an arm-chair in the sitting-room, reading a newspaper.

"Hello, Dad," said William. Mr. Brown grunted.

William resisted the temptation to launch at once into his main theme. He must pave the way to it by finesse and casual small-talk.

"Anythin' int'restin' in the paper, Dad?" he said, standing behind his father's chair and craning his head over his shoulder.

"D'you mind not breathing down my neck, my boy?" said Mr. Brown patiently.

"IF YOU GIVE ME THE MONEY, I PROMISE I'LL LEAD A
BETTER LIFE," SAID WILLIAM.

William withdrew from the chair and went to the
window.

"It's a nice day, isn't it, Dad?" he said.

"D'you mind not standing in my light, my boy?"
said Mr. Brown a little less patiently.

"They're comin' tonight, Dad," said William,
abandoning finesse, "an'—gosh! They're absolutely
smashing! They ride standin' up on their horses'
backs goin' at lightnin' speed an' they jump from one
horse to another an' they ride standin' on each other's
shoulders—*three* of them——"

Mr. Brown heaved a deep sigh and lowered his paper.

"May I ask what you're talking about, William?"
he said.

"The Wonder Cossacks, Dad. They're comin' tonight to Five Acre Meadow. They're *smashing*, Dad.
They—they do a cavalry charge an' they pick things

up from the ground, bendin' down from their horses an' bendin' back like a flash an' they jump over each other an'—an' they're *wizard*, Dad."

"What exactly is all this leading up to, William?" said Mr. Brown.

"Well, you see," said William., "it's a shillin' entrance an' Ginger an' me haven't got any money."

"Now, listen, William," said Mr. Brown, laying down his paper and assuming his rôle of paterfamilias, "you must learn to take the consequences of your actions. Your pocket money has been stopped as a punishment for breaking a window and, if I gave you the money to go to this riding display, there'd be no point in the punishment, would there?"

William considered.

"Well, I could sort of *repent* without a punishment, couldn't I? People often do in books. . . . An' listen, Dad. . . . If you give me the money to go to it, I promise I'll lead a better life. An'—*Gosh!* It'd be only two shillin's for Ginger an' me."

"No, William." Mr. Brown picked up his paper with an air of finality. "I'm sorry, but it's no use discussing it any further. As I said, you must learn to take the consequences of your actions."

"But, Dad—— Oh, gosh!"—as Robert entered the room—"some people jus' don't know what manners is. Buttin' in on other people what are havin' private conversations!"

"*Some* people," said Robert, "might look better if they brushed their hair and washed their faces and pulled their stockings up and tucked their shirts into their pants."

"Huh!" said William trying to instil into the ejaculation such scorn and contempt as to wither Robert completely.

Robert, however, remained unwithered. He took his stand on the hearth-rug and addressed his father.

"Going to golf this afternoon, Dad?" he said.

"No, my boy," said Mr. Brown. "I'm going to put some fertiliser on the chrysanthemum bed. It's one of those jobs I've been putting off for weeks, and I must really get down to it at last."

"Looks a bit like rain," said Robert, glancing out of the window.

"If it rains, I'll stain that new white-wood boot cupboard I bought," said Mr. Brown. "Another of those jobs I've been putting off and must get down to."

"Dad——" began William, who had thought of several fresh lines of argument in the meantime.

"Be quiet, William," said Mr. Brown. "Don't interrupt people when they're talking. . . . What are your plans, Robert?"

"I'm playing rugger this afternoon and then I'm going round to Roxana's to help lay some crazy paving."

William said "Huh!" again, but again Mr. Brown said, "Be quiet, William," and again Robert remained unwithered.

"She's making a sort of fancy garden," said Robert.

"What sort of fancy garden?" said Mr. Brown.

"Well, it started as an Italian garden because she got a garden ornament from somewhere, then it turned into a sunk garden because she saw one on the films and now someone's given her a job lot of bulbs and she's going to turn it into some sort of a Dutch garden."

"A double Dutch garden, presumably," said Mr.

Brown. "The craziness doesn't seem to stop at the paving."

"Anyway, she's having a working-party there this evening and everyone's going to help lay the paving and I'm taking along the cement for it."

"Dad," said William earnestly, "if you'll let me have two shillin's for me an' Ginger to go to the Wonder Cossacks, you can do anythin' else you like to me as a punishment about the window. You can pull all my teeth out, if you like, same as they did in hist'ry or—or screw my thumbs or—or rack me or—or scalp me or——"

"William," said Mr. Brown, "I should be glad if you would kindly not mention that horse show again. I've said my last word on the subject and it is now closed."

"I got a very good snapshot of her," said Robert, "standing by the sundial with the light shining on her hair. I don't know whether you'd care to see it, Dad. She really has rather lovely hair. . . ."

"Huh!" said William.

"Lunch is ready," called Mrs. Brown from the dining-room.

"Well, did you get anythin' out of yours?" said Ginger when the two met after lunch.

"No, he was in an awful temper," said William. "Wouldn't even listen. Wouldn't even bother to pull my teeth out or scalp me instead, though I said he could. I bet I'd get on all right without 'em. I wouldn't be always havin' to brush my hair an' clean my teeth, anyway. I once heard of an old man that could crack nuts with his gums an' I bet I'd soon get like that. Did yours give you anythin'?"

"No. Jus' snapped my head off. Said I'd got to learn to take the consequences of my actions."

"So did mine. . . . Gosh, aren't they mean! They spend pounds an' *pounds* on useless things like curtains an' carpets an' won't even spend two shillin's to help their sons to lead a better life. I *told* him I'd lead a better life if he gave me two shillin's an' he didn't seem to mind whether I did or not. Serve him right if I turn out a crim'nal. I've a good mind to turn out one jus' to show him."

"Yes, but what are we goin' to do about the Wonder Cossacks?" said Ginger. "They're puttin' up a tent an' I've seen the horses comin' along an' everyone's goin' to it . . . *everyone!*"

"Well, we're jolly well not goin' to not go to it jus' 'cause they're too mean to want their sons to lead better lives," said William firmly. "Fancy puttin' carpets an' curtains an' things before your own children! . . . I remember he paid fifteen shillin's once for a garden spray. Gosh! We could've seen the Wonder Cossacks"—he paused and wrinkled his brow in mental effort—"seven an' a half times for that."

"Yes, but how're we goin' to get that two shillin's for tonight?" said Ginger. "That's the question."

"We'll earn it," said William after a moment's consideration. "All the grown-ups I know get money by earnin' it, so it mus' be jolly easy. I bet when I start doin' all those things I'm goin' to do when I grow up, I'll have enough money to buy a whole circus, with elephants an' lions an' a performin' seal, an' I'll have a——"

"Yes, but listen," interrupted Ginger, trying to stop the flight of William's imagination before it had got completely beyond control, "what we've got to think of now is how to get that two shillin's for tonight."

"I've told you," said William a little testily. "By earnin' it. By doin' things for people an' gettin' paid for it. I once met a boy that'd got ten shillin's in one day, doin' things for people an' gettin' paid for it. Why, we could go to the Wonder Cossacks an' have dozens of ice creams an' buy that jet bomber we saw in that shop in Hadley an'——"

"Yes, but how'll we *start*?" said Ginger, making another effort to bring William down to earth. "We've got to start with somethin' *def'nite*."

William knit his brows into a complicated pattern as he grappled with the problem.

"What about your aunt?" he said at last. "Didn't you say she was tryin' to get a gardener?"

"Yes, but——"

"We'll go an' do a bit of gardenin' for her then. We'll do it cheap. We'll only charge a shillin' an hour each. . . . Let's see. . . . There's five hours before the Wonder Cossacks begins. . . . That's ten shillin's. Gosh! We can buy that submarine as well as the jet bomber."

"Well, let's go 'n' ask her first," said Ginger who took a less roseate view of their prospects than his friend.

"All right. Come on," said William.

A prolonged and thunderous knocking brought Ginger's aunt to the door.

"What on *earth's* the matter?" she said.

William bared his teeth in his polite smile.

"Nothin'," he said reassuringly. "It's quite all right. There's nothin' for you to worry about. We've jus' come to do a bit of gardenin' for you, that's all, an' we only charge a shillin' an hour each an' we can come straight away an' we can stay till about seven. We thought you'd like us to do a bit of gardenin' for you."

The grimness of Ginger's aunt's expression did not relax.

"As you did last time, I suppose," she said severely. "Pulling up all my precious mesembrianthemum seedlings!"

"Oh, that!" said William, a little disconcerted by the reminder. "Oh, yes, I'd jus' forgot that for the minute. . . . Well, that was a long time ago. It was *weeks* ago. We're a lot older than that now an' we've got a bit more sense. An'—an' those—messy flowers——"

"Mesembrianthemum," said Ginger's aunt coldly.

"Well, yes, whatever they are," agreed William. "Well, they *looked* like weeds. I bet anyone'd have taken 'em for weeds, same as we did. I bet they *were* weeds, too. I bet you'd *paid* for those—those messy flower seeds——"

"Mesembrianthemum," said Ginger's aunt.

"Yes, those," agreed William. "Well, I bet you'd *paid* for seeds of them 'an the man gave you weed seeds by mistake. I bet——"

"Good-bye," said Ginger's aunt in a tone of icy dismissal, and closed the door with a sharp snap.

"Well, *that* wasn't much good," said Ginger. "I'd got a sort of feelin' it wouldn't be."

"She jus' doesn't know anythin' about gardenin'," said William. "Doesn't know weeds from messy-what-she-said flowers. I'm jolly sorry for her trying

H

to get things to grow in her garden an' not knowin' weeds from those ole messy things. Anyway," with a return of his self-confidence, "there's lots of other things we can do to earn money. I'm jolly glad she wouldn't have us. I'm jolly glad I've not got to waste an afternoon gardenin' for someone what doesn't know weeds from messy-whatever-it-is."

"What else is there we can do?" said Ginger.

Once more William's brow corrugated itself in search of inspiration and cleared as inspiration came.

"Old Miss Forrester!" he said. "She pays to get that old dog of hers taken for walks. Let's go 'n' take the old dog for a walk. I bet she'll give us two shillin's for it."

"We did it once before an' it turned out wrong," said Ginger vaguely.

William cast his mind back over the last few months. The last few months contained so many things that had turned out wrong that it was difficult to disentangle them.

"I bet it'll be all right," he said. "I bet she'll be jolly grateful to us. Let's try, anyway. . . . Her house is jus' near. She's a bit deaf so let's give her a louder knock than ordin'ry."

The shattering tattoo on her knocker brought Miss Forrester to the door with a startled expression on her prim old face.

"Yes, yes? What is it? What is it?" she said.

"Can we take your dog for a walk?" said William, raising his voice, in consideration of her deafness, to a bellow that seemed to shatter the whole neighbourhood and that made even Miss Forrester blench and wince.

"We'll do it cheap. We won't charge more'n two shillin's."

The dim short-sighted eyes peered intently at the two boys, and the old lady's expression of nervousness was replaced by one of severity.

"*You're* the boys who took him out before," she said.

"Yes, I b'lieve we did," said William vaguely, "but we don't mind takin' him out again. We——"

"Took him *ratting*," said Miss Forrester, her voice quivering with indignation. "Brought him home in a *shocking* state! How *dare* you come here again!"

Vague memories in William's mind became clearer. ... A mud-bespattered dog with a bleeding ear, barking hilariously, leaping up exuberantly. ...

"Yes, but he enjoyed it," he said. "He had a jolly good time."

"Go away at once, you naughty boys, and never come here again," said Miss Forrester as she closed the door.

"*Well!*" said William. "Did you ever hear of anythin' like that? We gave that dog the best time it'd ever had in its life, an' we get no gratitude for it at all. Gosh! We ought to've charged *extra* for takin' it rattin'."

"I remember now," said Ginger. "She wouldn't give us anythin' at all. She was mad with us."

"Well, it jolly well serves her right that we won't take it rattin' again," said William, making a slight mental adjustment of the situation, "an' we won't now, not even if she comes beggin' us on her knees to take it rattin'."

"Well, she's not likely to," said Ginger, "an' we aren't any nearer gettin' that two shillin's."

"Well, we've only tried two things," said William. "There's *hundreds* more to try."

"What is there?" said Ginger.

"Well, there's—— Gosh! Don't you remember? Mrs. Pelham pays people to do shoppin' for her."

"We did it once. . . ."

"Yes, an' we brought back the right change an' the right things an' didn't forget anythin'."

"Yes, but somethin' went wrong with it—I forget jus' what," said Ginger. "She wouldn't give us any money."

"Well, we'll jolly well see she gives us some this time," said William firmly.

"I bet she won't give us two shillin's."

"We'll start by askin' for two shillin's," said William, "an' if she won't give it us we'll take less. We'll take one an' six."

"Or a shillin'."

"Yes, or sixpence."

"Even a penny would help."

"Yes, it'd be a start," agreed William. "Well, come on!"

Mrs. Pelham answered their knock, holding a baby in one arm and a mop in the other.

"Yes, what do you want?" she said with a bright inquiring smile.

"Please can we do some shoppin' for you?" said William. "We don't charge much. We only charge two shillin's, but if you've not got two shillin's we don't mind takin' sixpence an'——"

Mrs. Pelham looked at them more closely and the bright inquiring smile faded from her face.

"You did some shopping for me once before," she said.

"Well, yes, I b'lieve we did," said William.   "We're jolly good at doin' shoppin'.   We——"

"You crossed the river by the stepping stones, though there was no need to cross the river at all, and dropped the whole basket of groceries into the water."

"Well, yes," said William as that scene, too, loomed out of the mists of the past.   "Well, yes, I remember now we did, but we fished 'em all out.   It wasn't deep where we dropped 'em an' we fished 'em all out an' we dried 'em.   We dried 'em in the sun.   I bet it did 'em *good* havin' a bit of a wash an' bein' dried in the sun.   I bet——"

He stopped short as the door closed sharply in his face.

"People don't seem to have any *manners* nowadays," he said severely.   "Shuttin' the door before you've finished talkin' to them!"

"Well, that wasn't much good, either," said Ginger.

"N-no," agreed William as they walked slowly down the road.   "Well, it's their look-out if they don't want a bit of good gardenin' or shoppin' or dog-takin'-out done."

"It's ours, too," said Ginger gloomily.   "I don't see it's much use goin' on tryin' to get that two shillin's."

For a moment or two William seemed infected by Ginger's pessimism, then he brightened.

"*Tell* you what!" he said.

"Yes?"

"I think those things didn't come off 'cause we sort of asked first an' gave them a chance of sayin' 'no'.   I mean, they seemed to have got a funny sort of idea that we'd make a mess of them . . . but if we could *do* somethin' for someone without askin' first an' then *show* them how well we'd done it, I bet they'd be so grateful they'd give us that two shillin's straight away . . . Yes, that's what we'll do. We'll *do* somethin' for someone without askin' an' I bet they'll be so grateful they'll give us *more'n* two shillin's."

"Yes, but what'll we do for who?" said Ginger.

"We've got to think that out next," said William with a slight note of irritation in his voice. "I can't think of *everythin*' at the same time. I'm only yuman. I've only got one head. I'm not an octopus. Well, it's news to *me* if I'm an octopus."

"A' right," said Ginger apologetically, "but we've got to get it fixed up quick, 'cause——"

A light had broken out over William's sombre countenance.

"Gosh!" he said. "I've jus' thought of somethin'. My father was goin' to stain that cupboard of his brown if it rained an' it hasn't rained, so he won't have done it, so if we do it for him he'll be jolly grateful an' give us two shillin's."

"Um-m," said Ginger reflectively. "Well, have you got any brown paint?"

"No. Have you?"

"No."

"Well, he jus' wants it a brown colour. He didn't say paint. He jus' said 'stain', so I 'spect anythin'd do. There's a bottle of cough mixture in the medicine cupboard. It's a jolly good brown. We might try that."

"Yes, an' someone'll get a cough while we're do'in it an' go'n' look for the cough mixture an' we'll get into another row."

"Y-yes. . . ." Once again thought wove a complicated pattern on William's brow . . . then inspiration came and it cleared. "I've got another idea. There's a bottle of something called Hair Tonic of Dad's in the bathroom that's a sort of brown."

"Better leave your father's things alone," said Ginger apprehensively.

"Yes," agreed William regretfully. "P'r'aps we had. He might get ragin' mad an' he's like someone out of hist'ry when he gets ragin' mad."

"Listen, I've jus' thought of somethin'," said Ginger. "I once read a story where a man wanted to disguise himself as a gipsy an' he stained himself with walnut."

"Gosh!" said William, staggered by the simplicity of the idea. "Walnut? Jus' ordin'ry walnuts off trees?"

"I s'pose so," said Ginger.

"Well, we've got to get some ordin'ry walnuts off trees, then. We——"

They stopped simultaneously. They were passing Miss Milton's house. Over the hedge that divided her garden from the road stretched the branch of a large walnut tree.

"Come on!" said William.

It was not the first time that William and his friends had rifled that branch of Miss Milton's walnut tree. It was indeed one of their regular autumnal activities. So far this autumn they had been too busy with various other pursuits to give much attention to it, but now William took a stone from the road and hurled it into the tree with a skill born of long practice. Two small wizened-looking walnuts fell into the road.

"I bet they won't be enough to do a whole cupboard," said William, picking them up, inspecting them critically and putting them into his pocket. "I'll have another shot."

"Well, look out," said Ginger. "Her garden frame's just over the hedge, you know."

"I know *that*," said William, "an' I'm not such a rotten shot as to go throwin' stones that'll fall on her garden frame. Jus' watch me!"

He took up another stone and hurled it into the branch. There came the sound of the rustle of leaves, followed by the tinkle of breaking glass.

"Gosh!" said William with a gasp of horror. "Let's get away quick."

But it was too late. Miss Milton was already emerging from the gate, her face tense with anger.

"So it's *you* who are throwing stones at my garden frame, William Brown!" she said. "I might have known."

"I didn't throw 'em *at* your garden frame, Miss Milton," said William, "an' I'm sorry it got broke. We were only tryin' to get a few walnuts jus' to stain this cupboard 'cause of tonight. . . . Gosh, Miss Milton, they ride three of 'em on each other's shoulders an'—an'——"

"An' *swoop* things up from the ground at lightnin' speed," said Ginger, "an'—an'——"

"An' you ought to see the cavalry charge. They stop dead in a straight line an'——"

"An' start off again an'——"

"An' jump right over each other an'——"

"Be *quiet*," said Miss Milton. "I don't know what you're talking about, but I shall write a strong letter of complaint to your fathers. You've *ruined* my garden frame."

"Gosh, Miss Milton, don't write to our fathers, *please*," said William. "We're sorry about your frame an' it was my fault, an' I don't know what made that stone go a diff'rent way to what I threw it. I bet it mus' be somethin' to do with the atom bomb. Somethin' got out into the air out of the atom bomb and—and sort of *mesmerised* it.... Listen, Miss Milton. I'll mend your garden frame. Honest, I will. I bet I can find a bit of glass an' I know where there's a tube of glue an', honest, I'll mend it if you won't write to our fathers. I'll——"

"Will you be *quiet*, William Brown!" said Miss Milton, raising her voice to stem the tide of William's eloquence. "I shall most *certainly* write to your fathers. As if I hadn't enough trouble on my hands today with my darling Charlemagne escaped and gone Heaven knows where!"

Charlemagne was Miss Milton's parrot—a decrepit fowl of mildewed moth-eaten appearance, who was content generally to doze away his time in the intervals of devouring huge slices of the sponge cake for which he had a morbid passion.

"I always let him out of his cage for a few minutes in the morning," went on Miss Milton, as if talking to herself, "and I've no idea how the window came to be open. . . . And now *this* on the top of it! I only hope that you'll both be severely punished."

With that she set off down the road, her thin form still quivering with indignation. The two boys stood staring after her.

"Well, now *that's* all messed up too," said Ginger.

"No, it isn't," said William. "I'm not goin' to be put off by a little thing like that. I started out to get that two shillin's for the Wonder Cossacks an' I'm jolly well goin' to do it. I can't help her rotten old parrot 'scaping an' puttin' her in a bad temper. Gosh! If I was her parrot I'd jolly well escape, too. *An'* I wouldn't come back!"

"Our fathers are goin' to be mad," said Ginger.

"Well, she said she'd *write* to them, so that means they won't get the letters till tomorrow mornin', so I'm goin' to go into her old garden an' climb her old tree an' *get* those walnuts for stainin' the cupboard."

"Gosh! You're not goin' to go right into her garden, are you?" said Ginger in mingled horror and admiration.

"Yes, I am," said William. "We can get enough walnuts in no time if we climb the tree an' it'll take us all day throwin' stones at that branch. Anyway, I couldn't get into a worse row than I'm goin' to, so it doesn't matter what I do extra. An' I don't mind what happens to me tomorrow mornin' if I've been to see the Wonder Cossacks tonight. I wouldn't mind even bein' jellatined, same as they did in the French Revolution."

"I don't think it was jellatined," said Ginger thoughtfully. "I think it was another word but I've forgotten what."

"Well, whatever it was," said William. "I wouldn't mind bein' it tomorrow if I'd been to the Wonder Cossacks tonight. An' you needn't come with me if you don't want to."

"'Course I'll come," said Ginger, who was apt to

discourage William's more lawless adventures but never to the point of refusing to take part in them.

"All right. Come on."

Cautiously they entered the gate and began the ascent of the walnut tree. William went first, hoisting himself up from the back of the garden seat and scrambling recklessly from branch to branch. Ginger followed more slowly and carefully.

"I can see lots of walnuts up here," panted William. "The branches are gettin' a bit thin. There's a big bare patch here . . . but I bet I can manage it if I take my life in my hands. . . . There! I took my life in my hands an' managed it. It's easier now. . . ."

"I say, William!" said Ginger, a note of urgency in his voice.

"Yes?"

"She's comin' back. I can see her comin' back down the road. She mus' jus' have gone to the pillar box. Let's get down quick."

There was a short silence, broken by William's voice, which sounded rather small and seemed to come from a long way off.

"I can't . . . I'm stuck."

"Stuck?"

"Yes. I dunno how I got up that bare part, but I can't get down . . . I can't find anywhere for my feet. . . . I'm stuck. . . . Gosh! I may have to stay here for the rest of my life. You'd better get down if you can."

"No, I'll stay up here with you. . . . Let's freeze same as animals. P'r'aps if we don't move we'll look like part of the tree an' she won't notice."

"All right," said William. "I'll stretch out a bit an' try 'n' look like part of the branch."

THERE WAS A CRACKING OF TWIGS, A PIERCING SCREAM, AND WILLIAM AND GINGER, WITH CHARLEMAGNE BETWEEN THEM, ROLLED ON TO THE GRASS AT MISS MILTON'S FEET.

"So'll I."

"An' stop breathin'," said William. "I can hear you breathin' from here."

"Well, I've got to breathe to live, haven't I?" rejoined Ginger indignantly, then his voice sank again to an urgent whisper. "Look! She's comin' in at the gate . . . I bet she won't see us. . . ."

There came the click of the garden gate and the sound of Miss Milton's footsteps along the path. They stopped abruptly beneath the walnut tree, and Miss Milton's voice, shrill with indignation, reached the trespassers.

"Who are those boys up that tree? Can I believe my eyes, William Brown? Have you had the *audacity* to enter my garden and climb my tree after what I said to you?"

"Well, you see, Miss Milton," said William. "You see . . . I mean . . ."

While he searched wildly for some reason to explain his presence in the tree, Miss Milton's voice reached him again, upraised this time, to his amazement, not in anger but in gratitude.

"Oh, William, I've only just seen him. How good of you to go to his rescue!"

William had flattened himself against his branch and now, for the first time, he noticed Charlemagne, cowering sullenly, with drooping head and feathers, on the same branch a few feet away from him.

"You've nearly got him, dear boy," said Miss Milton in eager encouragement. "One more little effort. . . . Nothing rash, of course, but——"

"Go on, William," urged Ginger, who had now also seen the despondent bird. "Grab him by his neck."

"Gently, dear boy, gently!" said Miss Milton. "He's full of spirit. Don't antagonise him."

But Charlemagne's spirit, such as it was, had not survived his escapade. He gave a half-hearted peck at William's hand as he secured him, then contented himself by muttering "Oh, my goodness!" as William turned to contemplate the drop that yawned beneath him.

"If you let yourself go, I'll try'n' catch you," offered Ginger adding, "I'm stronger than what I look."

"Gently, gently, dear boy!" said Miss Milton again. "No risk to life and limb, I pray! By the way, if you could just move your finger out of Charlemagne's yet. . . ."

"Oh, my sainted aunt!" muttered Charlemagne.

"I think I can do it," said William, clutching the trunk with knees and arms and still keeping a firm hold on Charlemagne's neck. "I'll take my life in my hands again."

There was the sound of the cracking of twigs, a piercing scream from Charlemagne, a long wail from Miss Milton, and William and Ginger, with Charlemagne firmly pinioned between them, rolled on to the grass at Miss Milton's feet.

"Gosh!" panted William.

"Blimey!" said Charlemagne.

"Pardon him, dear," said Miss Milton in a shaking voice. "He doesn't often use bad language. I think he picked it up from the chimney sweep. You aren't hurt, I hope?"

"Only a bit bumped," said William, brushing his knees down and inspecting them with interest. "I've got a bruise startin' on this one—'least, it might be dirt—an' I've got a great c'lossal scratch on this one inches deep."

"Well, as long as no bones are broken . . ." said Miss Milton.

"I don't know about bones," said William, "'cause you can't see 'em. I 'spect they're all broke if you could see 'em."

"I don't think so, dear," said Miss Milton, watching him as he sprang into the air and made an ineffectual grab at a walnut that hung on one of the lower branches. "Now come into the house and help me settle poor Charlemagne. . . . Of course, I'll make no complaint to your fathers about the garden frame after your noble rescue of my poor little pet." William and Ginger murmured their thanks. "I'm sure you'll never do anything so barbarous and uncivilised again, will you?"

"No," said William.

"You betcher life!" said Charlemagne with a sardonic snort.

Miss Milton looked pained.

"I'm afraid he's picked up one or two vulgar expressions from the tradespeople," she said. "He *can* say some quite nice things, but he doesn't often trouble. I've tried to teach him nursery rhymes—'Little Miss Muffet' and 'Little Jack Horner'—but he didn't seem interested. . . . Come along into the kitchen, children. I can't think why the darling flew away. I do all I can to make him happy, but sometimes I'm afraid he finds me rather dull company."

"You're telling *me*!" said Charlemagne bitterly.

She brought Charlemagne's cage into the kitchen and fastened him into it. He settled down on his perch with a resigned shrug.

"I think I'll give him a little warm milk," said Miss Milton. "His nerves must be simply *shattered*. And he's very fond of sponge cake. . . . Will one of you get the sponge cake that's in the larder while I attend to his milk? It's on the middle shelf, next to those bottles of walnut ketchup."

"Walnut *what*?" said William excitedly.

"Ketchup, dear. . . . And be as quick as you can. He must be faint with hunger."

William emerged from the larder, carrying the sponge cake and wearing a thoughtful air.

"And now perhaps you'd better go away, children," said Miss Milton, as she placed a saucer of warm milk in the cage. "I think he needs perfect quiet for a bit, don't you, my pet?"

"You naughty boys!" said Charlemagne in a voice so like Miss Milton's that even Miss Milton looked startled. Then he ejaculated "Blimey!" again and began to dance about in his saucer of milk with a slightly inebriated air.

"I'd like to give you boys some little reward for your kind rescue of him," said Miss Milton. "I never give money to children on principle, but if there's any little thing you'd like as a gift. . . ."

"Can we have some walnut ketchup, please?" said William.

"Walnut ketchup?" said Miss Milton. "What a curious taste! But I have plenty, so you can take a bottle of it if you wish."

"Thanks," said William. He vanished into the larder and reappeared with a bottle of walnut ketchup. There was a new expression of purpose on his face. "Come on, Ginger. G'bye, Miss Milton."

"Good-bye, boys," said Miss Milton.

"Little Miss Muffet sat on a Christmas pie," sang Charlemagne on a quavering, uncertain note.

"Good ole Charlie," said Ginger as the two set off down the road. "He got us out of *that* mess all right."

"Yes, an' he didn't half peck my hand," said William, adding "Blimey!" with a rather self-conscious air.

"You oughtn't to say that," said Ginger virtuously. "It's a bad word."

"If a parrot can say it, I can," said William. "There's nothin' wrong in imitatin' the notes of birds. People do it on the wireless an' get *paid* for it. It's no diff'rent from sayin' 'Cuckoo'. It's the note of a parrot an' I'm jolly well goin' to imitate it."

"Well, what did you want that walnut ketchup for?" said Ginger, finding William's arguments, as usual, unassailable.

"To stain that cupboard of Dad's, of course, an' put him in a good temper so's we can go to the Wonder Cossacks. It's a jolly good idea, gettin' that catchup stuff. 'Catchup' mus' mean some sort of stain. I bet it's French or somethin' for 'stain'. Well, stands to reason it mus' be."

"Y-yes, I s'pose it is," said Ginger doubtfully. "She said it had a curious taste."

"Yes, I bet it has, too," said William. "I once swallowed a bit of paint by mistake an' it had a *jolly* curious taste, blimey!"

"You'll get into a row sayin' it," said Ginger.

"No, I won't. I keep tellin' you that there's nothin' wrong imitatin' birds' notes. Good people do it. . . . Come on! Let's go home an' do that cupboard.

I'm beginnin' to feel that we're goin' to get to the Wonder Cossacks after all, aren't you?"

"Well," said Ginger, "in a way I am an' in a way I'm not."

"Oh, come on!" said William impatiently.   "Let's run."

They ran till they were in sight of William's house, then slackened their pace and approached the garden slowly and cautiously.   The form of Mr. Brown could be seen, stooping over the chrysanthemum bed, taking handfuls of powder from a large paper bag and scattering it over the soil.

"Come on, let's go in without him seein' us," said William.   "I want it to be a s'prise.   If it's a s'prise I bet he'll be so pleased he'll give us that two shillin's straight off, but if he knew we were goin' to do it he'd stop us, 'cause he wouldn't know how pleased he'd be if it was a s'prise."

Silently the two crept upstairs to Mr. Brown's dressing-room and stood for a moment surveying the white-wood boot cupboard.

"There's a lot of it to do," said William.   "Hope there'll be enough walnut stuff."

"We might find some brown shoe polish or somethin' to finish it off with if there isn't," said Ginger.

"Yes, we'll find somethin'," said William carelessly. "Let's start with the walnut stuff anyway."   He took the bottle from his pocket and put it on the top of the cupboard.   "What about a paint brush?   Have you got a paint brush?"

"No.   Have you?"

"No. . . .   *Tell* you what!   I'll use my handkerchief."

"IT'LL LOOK BETTER WHEN IT'S FINISHED," SAID WILLIAM.
"WE'VE TAKEN A LOT OF TROUBLE OVER IT, DAD."

"You'll get it in an awful mess."

William drew a sodden, mud-coloured length of material from his pocket.

"It won't do it any harm," he said. "It's the one I used sievin' for gold in the stream this mornin'. . . . Go on! You shake a splodge of the walnut stuff on it an' I'll rub it in."

With this division of labour they worked in silence for some time.

"It's makin' it brown all right," said William at last, a little doubtfully. "Well, it's darkenin' it, anyway."

"It's a bit patchy," said Ginger critically, "an' some patches are browner than others."

"Well, try blobbing the stuff straight on to the

wood," said William, "an' I'll rub it in with the hand-kerchief."

Again they worked in silence for some minutes.

"I think it looks all right, don't you?" said William uncertainly.

"I'm not sure," said Ginger, surveying the blotchy expanse with a critical frown that changed to a look of apprehension as his gaze wandered further afield. "I say! A lot's gone on the carpet. An' it's all over you."

"I 'spect it'll clean off," said William carelessly.

He paused to look out of the window. Mrs. Brown was entering the gate with a laden shopping basket. Mr. Brown left his gardening operations to join her. They walked towards the house together.

"Come on," said William. "Let's try 'n' get it finished before he comes upstairs."

The voices of Mr. and Mrs. Brown rose to them from the hall.

"Had a successful afternoon's gardening, dear?" said Mrs. Brown.

"On the whole," said her husband, "but the fertiliser seems to have acquired a most peculiar consistency. It's been a damp summer, of course. A good thing to have got it used up. . . . Well, I'll go upstairs and wash my hands."

"I'll have tea ready in a few minutes," said Mrs. Brown.

"Gosh, he's comin' upstairs," whispered William. He looked at the smeared and patchy top of the cup-board with a sudden sinking of his heart. "Splodge a bit more on quick . . . I bet it's all right *really*. I bet it looks a bit sort of funny to us 'cause we've jus' done it. I bet it'll look all right when it's dry. . . . Anyway, we've taken a lot of trouble over it, so it *mus'* be all right."

Mr. Brown's footsteps reached the top of the stairs and paused.

"What are you boys doing in my dressing-room?" he said.

"We—we've got a sort of s'prise for you, Dad," said William.

"A surprise?" Mr. Brown's voice lacked the note of gratitude and pleased expectancy that William had hoped for. "What d'you mean, a surprise?"

Footsteps sounded along the passage and Mr. Brown appeared in the doorway. There was a silence during which he looked at the cupboard, strong emotions chasing each other over his purpling countenance.

"It'll look better when it's finished," said William hastily, trying to use what arguments he could before the power of speech returned to Mr. Brown. "You said you wanted it stained brown, so we thought we'd do it for a nice surprise for you."

"We hoped you'd be pleased, Mr. Brown," said Ginger.

"We've taken a lot of trouble over it, Dad."

Then the power of speech returned to Mr. Brown and the house rocked with his wrath.

". . . Are you out of your senses? Don't you have any lucid intervals at all? . . . Filthy smears all over my new boot cupboard . . . Of all the imbecile things to do . . .! No one but a maniac would mistake a bottle of walnut ketchup for a bottle of walnut stain. . . . And why stop at the boot cupboard? Did you never think of hacking up the dressing-table or smashing the mirror . . .?"

It was like a raging torrent, engulfing the faint excuses that William and Ginger continued to make. "We didn't *mean* any harm, Dad" . . . "We were *tryin'* to help, Mr. Brown. . . ."

It seemed as if the storm might have raged for ever, had not Mrs. Brown called from downstairs.

"What on *earth* is the matter, dear?"

Mr. Brown stopped to draw breath.

"The matter?" he called when he had drawn it. "I'll come down and tell you what the matter is." He turned to William. "I shouldn't allow you to go to that horse show affair now even if you had the money. You can stay up here till I've decided what to do to you."

With that he descended to the hall and gave his wife a full and colourful account of the state of his boot cupboard.

"The whole place *sodden* with the filthy stuff. I expect it's even on the ceiling if I'd thought of looking!"

"Oh, but, John," said Mrs. Brown with a smile, "don't be too hard on them. They didn't mean any harm."

"Didn't mean any harm!" exploded Mr. Brown. "Smearing the disgusting mixture all over the place and rubbing it in with a handkerchief that might have been used to clean out a pig-sty."

"But, John, I expect they were only trying to help."

"Trying to help! Of all the idiotic excuses that were ever invented! And walnut ketchup!"

"These mistakes are easily made, you know, John."

"Not by people in their right minds. The boy ought to be in a madhouse. He needs a sharp lesson and

I'll see that he gets it.   The state of that room beggars description."

"I'll go up and see exactly what they have done," said Mrs. Brown turning to the stairs.

Mr. Brown went into the sitting-room, relaxed in an easy chair and mopped his brow.

"Of all the——" he muttered.

Then the door opened and Robert entered.   His face looked tense and harassed.

"I say, Dad," he said, "do you know what's happened to that bag of cement that was in the garage?"

Mr. Brown sat up slowly and a thoughtful expression came into his face.

"Cement?" he said.

"Yes," said Robert, "there was half a bag of cement in the garage and I can't find it anywhere.   I want to take it to Roxana's for the crazy paving."

"Half a bag of cement?" repeated Mr. Brown in a dazed fashion.

"Yes," said Robert impatiently.   "It was left over from making those coal bunks last year, you know."

"I—er—I don't remember seeing half a bag of cement in the garage, Robert.   There was half a bag of fertiliser that I used on the chrysanthemums this afternoon."

Robert stared at him.

"Fertiliser?"

There came into Mr. Brown's face the look of one who holds at bay a suspicion he dares not face.   He gave a self-conscious cough.

"Yes, Robert . . . fertiliser."

"There wasn't any fertiliser in the garage," said

Robert. "We used the last of it on the roses. Don't you remember?"

Mr. Brown coughed again.

"Yes—er—now you mention it, I do remember."

"When you said you were going to put some on the chrysanthemums this afternoon, I thought you must have bought some more . . ." Robert's face grew blank with slowly dawning horror. "Dad, you've *not* used the cement on the chrysanthemums, have you?"

"I—I really don't know, Robert," said Mr. Brown. "I certainly *thought* it was fertiliser, but I do remember, now you mention it, that we used the last of the fertiliser on the roses and that there was some cement left over from the coal bunks."

Robert's face was contorted by anguish.

"Oh, *really*, Dad! And Roxana's *counting* on me for the cement. I mean, the whole party's there to help lay the paving but I *definitely* promised to bring the cement along with me, and all the shops will be shut now . . . I shouldn't mind if it were anyone but Roxana . . . but—well, she's the most wonderful girl I've ever known in my life and I hate to let her down. I simply can't think how you could mistake cement for fertiliser, Dad."

By a supreme effort, Mr. Brown retained something of his dignity.

"I'm sorry, Robert," he said. "I didn't mean to cause you any inconvenience. I was only trying to help the family in general. I mean, your mother—and you, if it comes to that—like to have the garden looking nice and—well, I put in a lot of hard work on it. These mistakes are easily made."

"Yes, I'm sorry, Dad," said Robert. "I didn't mean to fly out. It was just a bit of a blow, that's all. . . . But I think the Jamesons have some cement. I'll go round there and see."

He went out, colliding with Mrs. Brown in the doorway and dashed off in the direction of the Jamesons' house.

"Whatever's the matter with Robert?" said Mrs. Brown.

"Oh—er—these young people get excited over trifles, you know," said Mr. Brown evasively.

"John, you were quite right about William," she said. "He's made a *shocking* mess. I quite agree that he needs teaching a sharp lesson."

"Oh, I don't know," said Mr. Brown. "The boy meant no harm. He was probably only trying to help."

"The *idiocy* of thinking that walnut ketchup was a walnut stain!"

"These little mistakes are easily made," said Mr. Brown.

"But, John, you said——"

"I know, I know," said Mr. Brown. "One's apt to form hasty and ill-considered judgments. I'll go up and have a word with them."

It was not often that William faced defeat, but he was facing it now.

"We shan't get to see those Wonder Cossacks, Ginger," he was saying. "I jus' can't b'lieve it's true, but it is. . . . Gosh! It's worse than the end of the world."

"An' they may never come again," said Ginger. "Never all the rest of our lives."

There came the sound of Mr. Brown's footsteps ascending the stairs. The two boys looked at each other apprehensively.

"Here he is!" said William gloomily, "an' I bet it *is* goin' to be worse than the end of the world, too."

"P'r'aps I'd better be goin' . . ." murmured Ginger.

Mr. Brown entered the room. He wore a slight— only a very slight—air of embarrassment.

"Well, boys," he said genially, "what about this Wonder Cossack show?"

William gaped at him, open-mouthed, his mind a confusion of amazement, incredulity, hope and joy.

"Gosh, Dad!" he said at last. "Do you mean you're goin' to let us go?"

Mr. Brown smiled a little sheepishly.

"I think I'd like to go myself," he said. "Let's all three go and forget our troubles."

"Blimey!" said William, adding hastily, "it's a bird note, Dad, same as 'cuckoo'."

"Gosh, Mr. Brown!" said Ginger in a voice so charged with emotion that it was little more than a squeak.

"Better clean yourselves up a bit," said Mr. Brown, looking down at the two dishevelled, ketchup-stained figures.

"Yes, we will," said William. "An'—we're sorry about that cupboard, Dad."

Mr. Brown waved the apology aside.

"These little mistakes will happen, my boy," he said.

THE END